ANTIQUE TRAGEDY

A DOTTY SAYERS ANTIQUE MYSTERY

VICTORIA TAIT

KANGA PRESS

A Kanga Press Publication © 2022

Cover Design by Daniela Colleo of StunningBookCovers.com
Editing Allie Douglas

For more information visit VictoriaTait.com

CHAPTER ONE

Twenty-nine-year-old, Dotty Sayers, stared at the flashing curser on her computer screen.

It was the first week in January and she was sitting at her desk in the office-cum-reception area of Akemans auction house, in the British Cotswolds.

In the corner of the room, her blue quilted jacket was hanging on the coat stand, dripping from the rain she'd run through earlier as she dashed from her car. Her bob of highlighted-blonde hair hung limply as it dried.

The door leading into the adjoining three-story antiques centre, converted from a nineteenth-century flour mill, opened and a smiling Gilly Wimsey came in.

Gilly, who ran Akemans antiques centre, pushed her orange-rimmed glasses up her nose and said cheerfully, "Morning, Dotty. I see you're already busy. Cup of tea?" She brushed an unruly orange curl away from her face.

Dotty stared vaguely at Gilly as she passed her desk, heading to the back of the small office where she switched on the electric kettle.

Dotty became aware of voices entering from the auction room. She closed her eyes and shook her head, trying to clear the fug inside it.

Gilly placed a mug of tea on her desk and said, "There you are. I hope that'll cheer you up."

"Gillian, do you have a minute?" asked David Rook. He was an intelligent-looking gentleman with short grey hair, a high, pronounced forehead, a salt and pepper moustache and a trim beard.

He often visited the Middle East and Dotty presumed from his darker skin tone that he had originated from the area. She was careful not to catch his large dark eyes, which were ever watchful.

Dotty looked down at the papers on her desk and the list of items from the previous auction. She needed to check them against the computer system and chase up any items which had not yet been paid for or collected.

The auction had been held between Christmas and New Year and, although she had been given time off and hadn't attended, she'd heard the sale was successful. But now she needed to prepare for what looked like being a full January auction.

Dotty heard Georgina - known to everyone as George - Carey Boyd, who ran Akemans auction house, mutter words including, "Lack of concentration,", "world of her own,", and "busy".

Tuning into the conversation between George, David and Gilly, she heard Gilly reply, "Gilmore's arrest really shook her. And I don't think it is purely down to his forged painting scam. She believed he felt something for her, and she was excited about their trip to Vienna. To find out Gilmore was going to use her as a mule to smuggle stolen paintings … Well, it's betrayal."

It certainly was. Dotty placed her hands around the mug of hot tea. Gilmore had been so charming and sophisticated, and everyone in the antiques world had respected him. And she'd been so taken in by his charms and thought that he'd liked her for … being herself.

She had no doubts now that her dead husband, Al, who had been fifteen years her senior, had only married her to keep house and cook his meals. A dutiful military wife. She sighed as her shoulders slumped.

"Dorothy," David called.

Woken from her introspection, Dotty raised her head and met David's dark eyes, which had a softness to them. "Have you completed your Modern Art course?"

To improve her professional knowledge, Dotty had enrolled in an Appreciation of Modern Art Short Course through Oxford University. She was supposed to have finished it by the end of the previous year, but her dissertation was still incomplete.

Dotty shook her head.

"Did you choose Picasso's paintings as the subject of your dissertation?" enquired David.

"His sculptures," Dotty replied in a hoarse voice. She sipped her tea.

"And how long will it take to complete it?" David pressed.

Dotty shrugged. "A couple of days."

Gilly stepped across and placed a hand on Dotty's shoulders. "Why don't you go home and finish it off? I'm looking forward to your award ceremony. I haven't worn my robes for years."

Dotty's eyes widened, and she blurted, "You were at Oxford University?"

Gilly laughed.

George approached Dotty's desk and revealed, "Despite her dishevelled appearance and chaotic manner, my sister has a sharp brain. Besides, someone needed to restore the family honour after my disgraceful return from Paris."

Dotty had recently found out that when George was a student she'd lived in Paris and had an affair with a married artist.

Gilly gave her sister a sympathetic, lopsided smile.

"So what do you say, Dorothy?" asked David. "Take the remainder of the week off to complete your coursework. And to make up for it, you can accompany me to the antique fair at Bath Showground on Saturday."

A trip to an antique fair. Now that sounded more interesting than sitting at her desk. And better than lying on the sofa all weekend stroking Earl Grey, her British Blue cat, even though he'd been a real comfort over the past couple of weeks.

She leaned back and, placing her hands on the paperwork on her desk, she asked, "But who's going to complete this?"

David smiled. "Marion is bored at home. No golf or tennis, and even our bridge games have dried up this month. Everyone is either heading to the Alps to go skiing or to the Caribbean for some winter sun. She'd be delighted to help out."

Marion, David's wife, was extremely efficient and usually assisted George on auction days. She'd stepped in to do Dotty's work at the December auction, so would be familiar with the auction lots.

Dotty looked from George to David to Gilly, whose hand still rested on her shoulder. "Thank you. It would be a relief to complete the course, and the sale information has been swimming around in front of me all morning."

"And the antique fair?" enquired David.

Dotty smiled weakly and replied, "Why not? I don't have anything better to do."

CHAPTER TWO

On Thursday morning, Dotty placed a cup of tea on the dark oak table that served as her desk in the small living room of her cottage.

She'd spent the rest of Wednesday, after being sent home, reading and researching Pablo Picasso and his sculptures.

She hadn't seen any of them in real life but was fascinated by reports by those who had that his works had an invigorating energy as well as freshness and creativity.

They showed a hunger to learn the essence of life itself, of truth, honesty and self-awareness. True self-awareness was something she realised she didn't have herself, but she wouldn't find it through art.

She switched on her laptop and sipped her tea.

Alone in her cottage, with Earl Grey occasionally padding through for attention, she felt a calmness that enabled her to concentrate on her work.

Outside she could hear the howl of the wind and the rain beating against her windows and she felt snug and secure in her living room, her cottage, her world.

Halfway through the morning, she stood up and made her way to the kitchen for a fresh cup of tea. She realised the rain had stopped and soft rays of sunshine were penetrating through the retreating grey clouds.

She worked for another hour until her tummy began to rumble. Lunch time.

As she pushed back her chair, her phone rang. She picked it up, noting David Rook's name on the caller ID.

"Hello, David."

"Sorry to bother you, Dorothy, but I have something which might be of interest."

"Go on," she replied uncertainly.

"I've just spoken to Chief Inspector Ringrose, who has been liaising with the British Museum and Customs and Excise. A private jet from UAE landed at Cotswold Airport yesterday and there is a collection of miniature handmade clay tiles amongst its cargo.

"But Customs and Excise are suspicious, and knowing little about antiquities, they contacted the British Museum. I'm known to the museum as an expert in Babylonian and Persian artefacts, so they've asked me to check the consignment, and I thought it might be an engaging activity for you."

Dotty glanced at her laptop. She'd definitely made progress this morning, and she was about to take a break for lunch.

As the rain had stopped, it might be nice to get out of the house for a few hours, and checking a consignment of tiles didn't sound like taxing work.

"Sure, that would be nice."

"Meet me at 2pm at the front gate of the airport and bring some ID. There will be passes waiting for us."

Dotty arrived at the main gate of the private airport, five miles to the south-west of Cirencester, at five minutes to two.

She was still spooked by the huge ghost-like passenger planes parked in a row beside the airport's chain-link fence, which towered above her as she'd approached the airport.

She'd been told that Cotswold Airport had a long runway which enabled such large planes to land, but they didn't take off again.

Instead, they were broken up for scrap and spares by a company located on the airfield.

David's vintage silver Mercedes braked to a stop behind her.

As they both climbed out of their cars, he remarked, "Excellent. Right on time. I'll sort out our passes and then you can follow me onto the airfield."

David returned from the guard hut and handed her a pass before getting in his car. He overtook her as the entrance barrier was raised and she followed him into the airport.

They turned immediately left and then right onto a service road with industrial units of various ages lining each side. He pulled up, and they parked in front of a modern unit with blueish-grey corrugated metal walls and a sloping roof.

A discrete square sign on the left of the unit revealed that it was occupied by HM Customs and Excise.

A man in his forties with a large oval face, wearing a blue uniform with gold buttons and piping on his sleeve, which made Dotty think of a Royal Navy officer, stepped through a white door to the side of the larger roller shutter.

He extended a hand and introduced himself as, "Greg Welford. You must be David Rook, the British Museum's antiquities expert."

David shook Greg's hand. "I am David. I work for a local company, but I've been asked by the British Museum and a local Chief Inspector to assist you. And I've brought my assistant, Dorothy."

Dotty and Greg shook hands before Greg instructed, "Follow me."

He led them inside the unit. At the far end there was a double-height brick wall with windows in it, and Dotty presumed these were offices. Several wooden pallets loaded with plastic-wrapped packages stood on the concrete floor of the unit.

Greg led them to an area containing several industrial packing benches with stained plywood tops and painted blue metal supports. Beside the first one, there were two open rectangular wooden crates with their lids lying across them at angles.

"The custom form claims these are miniature handmade clay tiles. And they do appear to be small clay tile shapes, but we don't think they are modern, and wanted an expert opinion."

Greg removed the lid from the first packing case, and David bent down. He removed a thick grey sheet of polystyrene. Beneath it he found individual compartments created by more sheets of polystyrene and in each a brown honeycomb-paper-wrapped package.

David lifted out one of the packages and placed it on the plywood packing bench. Carefully, he unwrapped the parcel to reveal a block of coffee-coloured stone with horizontal lines and symbols scratched on it. David whistled.

"What is it?" asked Dotty, feeling her body tense.

"A rare Ur dynasty clay tablet." David looked up at Greg. "You're right. This is not modern. It's over 4,000 years old."

"And worth more than £200?" Greg enquired.

David glanced down at the packing cases and replied, "I don't know how many we have in total, but we are talking thousands of pounds, potentially tens of thousands of pounds' worth of ancient relics."

He removed and unwrapped another parcel. The stone was lighter in colour and circular in shape. "I believe this one is inscribed with cuneiform script, one of the earliest recorded writing systems."

"Any idea where they originated from?" asked Greg.

"Probably southern Iraq. The British Museum recently handed over some other clay tablets to the National Museum of Iraq, as well as some priceless cylinder impressions sealed within their clay envelopes, which are believed to have been from a dig of an ancient city in that region."

"So we should hand these over to you?"

"You need to send them directly to the British Museum. I'm only a private consultant." David wore a pained expression.

"Do you not want them to go?" asked Dotty, somewhat confused. The clay tablets couldn't stay here and surely they were being illegally imported and couldn't be returned to their alleged owners.

David sighed. "The British Museum is committed to its fight against the illegal trade of historical artefacts."

"As indeed are we," added Greg.

"But while they acknowledge the damage caused by removing and shipping such objects outside their home countries, the museum itself continues to display many valuable international treasures. And arguably, some of those were looted. Consider the Rosetta Stone. The

Egyptian Government insists it was stolen and should be returned to them. And they have a point."

Dotty had seen the Rosetta Stone on a visit to the British Museum. It was much larger than these clay tiles, being over a metre in height, and at least 2,200 years old.

It was one of the museum's star attractions. She'd had to wait her turn as other visitors examined it in its glass display cabinet.

Greg cleared his throat. "It's not my job to get involved in politics. I'll box these up and send them to the British Museum. Thank you for your assistance."

"Any time," replied David politely.

David and Dotty left Greg and as they stepped outside the industrial unit, David asked, "Did you find that interesting?"

"Yes, but I wish we could have seen what else was in those boxes. What if there were more than just clay tiles?"

"I'll ask the British Museum if they can keep us updated and offer my services to them. Perhaps we'll have the opportunity to view the whole collection. My one concern is that it will be stored away in their basement rather than handed back to the Iraqi government."

"How did someone get hold of all those pieces?"

"Tens of thousands of objects disappeared during the invasion of Iraq in 2003, and only a small proportion have been returned."

"Where are they all?"

"Some are in museums, or stored away until they're authenticated, but many are in private collections. You see, as long as there are individuals who want to own beautiful objects from exotic sources, the underground antiquities trade will continue. Stolen cultural material and objects should be returned to their countries of origin. That would be the honest thing to do."

CHAPTER THREE

Saturday morning was bright but cold and a frost covered the landscape with a white sheen.

Dotty was relieved that she'd finished her dissertation on Pablo Picasso the previous evening and was now looking forward to her trip with David to the antique fair at Bath Showground.

David drove them both there in his vintage silver Mercedes.

"This fair is not as large as their summer one, which has hundreds of additional stalls outside on the showground. This weekend everything is inside the show buildings, but there will still be several thousand stalls."

Dotty blinked. The fair sounded rather overwhelming.

"Are you looking for anything in particular?" asked Dotty.

"No," replied David, staring at the road in front of him.

Why didn't she believe him?

They arrived at the wide expanse of showground, to the east of the historic Roman city of Bath, at a quarter past ten and parked on a gravel car park, already half-filled with a range of cars, vans and pickups.

Although there were no stalls outside, there were several food trucks and as they left the parking area, David asked, "Would you like a cup of tea before we begin?"

"Yes, please," Dotty replied.

They approached a white mobile trailer with a sign advertising 'Fresh Coffee'. A man with dark wavy hair, which reached the collar of his black polo neck jumper, was already sipping from a brown paper cup.

"Good morning, Didier," remarked David as he approached the man.

Dotty froze.

"I'm sure you remember Dorothy, from Akemans," continued David as he passed Didier and reached the coffee truck.

Didier turned to Dotty and smiled his wide, disarming smile, which didn't reach his eyes. "Of course. How are you? I understand you're still in the amateur detective game. I hope you're not here to arrest me."

Dotty had met Didier Vogt, an antiques dealer, at an auction the previous summer. They had both become entangled in a murder case when another auctioneer died at a charity triathlon.

Dotty also suspected Didier had been involved with a counterfeit furniture scam and had duped her into buying an expensive, but reproduced, Queen Anne table, but neither she nor the police could prove it.

She heard David murmur, "How are the girls?"

"I took them skiing in France for Christmas. I thought it better than being at home," acknowledged Didier.

David nodded as a young man in the coffee trailer said, in a bored tone, "Tea."

David ignored him and asked, "And have you spotted anything of interest today?"

"Like you, I've only just arrived, but I've been told there are some unusual objects in Hall 4."

"And a double espresso," the bored youth in the trailer called.

David nodded at Didier and turned to collect the two cups from the counter of the trailer. He walked back to Dotty, handed one of them to her and suggested, "Shall we begin?"

They entered the first hall, which was actually a large shed with a corrugated metal roof and exposed green metal roof trusses. It was enclosed by white-painted brick walls and packed with several rows of stalls.

People were everywhere and their chatter filled the building.

Dotty looked around, wondering where to start.

"Shall we begin on the left and work our way up and down the rows? The far end will be quieter and the stalls will have more space to sell their larger objects."

Dotty felt light-headed, so she sipped her tea before following David. They stood beside a stall selling an array of what Dotty thought of as vintage items rather than antiques. Three dolls in various states of dress were arranged next to a red, wind-up organ grinder box with a small soft toy monkey sitting on top.

In the corner, a pine unit with three shelves displayed porcelain bowls and figurines, and in front of it, there were glass bowls and plates decorated with flowers.

At the far end of the stall, a wooden display case with a sloping glass front exhibited smaller items, including silver, or silver-plated, salt and pepper shakers, condiments sets, and other trinkets.

"No new items can be sold at these fairs, and everything on display has to be out of production," explained David.

"That doesn't mean everything is old. Far from it. Several new stalls last year started selling early models of mobile phones, computers and gaming equipment. They're very popular, although I think most people are kicking themselves for throwing away their favourite Nokia phones and their handheld computer games from the 1980s."

They moved on to the next stall where two elderly ladies, one with straight, and the other with curly, white hair, were examining an old carved wooden duck.

They peered at its simple brown body and faded blue-painted beak through their glasses, as they leaned on their aluminium walking sticks.

The stall was dedicated to carved wooden animals, and Dotty wondered why the old ladies were attracted to the duck.

"Duck decoys are popular," the round-faced stallholder addressed the old women. "And that one will appeal to Americans as it's originally from Lake St Clair, in Michigan. I couldn't take less than

£500, but if you can get someone to buy it for more than that, I'll split the difference."

£500 for a wooden duck seems crazy, Dotty thought to herself.

"Come on, Edith." The lady with straight white hair nudged her companion. "We've work to do." She set off in a sprightly manner but suddenly slowed and used her walking stick to aid her across the hall.

David placed his hand on Dotty's back and guided her to the next stall.

He whispered, in an amused voice, "Don't be fooled by Ethel and Edith. They're two of the best low-level tricksters in the region. I've no idea if they actually need the money, but they enjoy the game."

"What game?" asked Dotty.

"They chose an item and agree a price with a stallholder, but instead of buying it themselves, they find someone else to buy it. Usually, a person who has already shown an interest in it. They begin a conversation near their target buyer, discussing the item and whether they should purchase it.

"They may say they saw a similar object a few weeks ago, and it sold for a much higher price, or that a renowned dealer is interested, so perhaps they should buy it first. That sort of thing. Their target thinks they're missing out on a good deal and they return to the stall and buy the item, but at an inflated price. Ethel and Edith are paid the difference by the stallholder.

"It's rather harmless and the stallholders sell an item, usually a valuable one, and those in the know are entertained by the old ladies' antics."

Dotty stared after the white-haired old ladies in bewilderment and sipped her tea as a man beside her asked, "What's the death?"

CHAPTER FOUR

David grabbed Dotty's half-empty paper cup before it hit the ground. Lukewarm tea sloshed over his hand and he deposited the cup in a nearby black plastic dustbin and returned to Dotty, wiping his hands with a navy-blue handkerchief.

"I can't go lower than 150," replied the stallholders, a lady with a streak of pink in her short brown hair.

David gently manoeuvred Dotty away from the stall as he explained, "The phrase 'what's the death?' is a common one at fairs. It means, what's your lowest price?"

"But I thought ..." Dotty's voice faltered.

"I know. The colour drained from your face. Do you want to sit down?"

Dotty's legs did feel weak, but she thought a walk would be better than sitting down. "Perhaps we can just keep moving."

They continued down the row of stalls.

David looked across at one before turning back to Dotty and whispering, "See that man?"

He pointed to a young man with short, dark, slightly wispy hair who was earnestly talking to an elderly stallholder. They shook hands and the younger man handed over a twenty-pound note and received a book in return.

Although Dotty was some distance away, she thought it was a cookery book with a torn blue cover and a picture of roast beef on the front.

"Nice buy," continued David in a hushed voice. "Let's follow him."

Dotty wasn't sure why David wanted to follow this young man, but intrigued, she complied.

He exited the hall by a side door, and they followed him into an adjoining shed with a similar layout to the one they had left.

The young man stopped at a bookstall and showed the woman stallholder the book he'd just bought. After a brief conversation, he handed over the book and received two twenty-pound notes from the stallholder.

"You've just witnessed Billy at work," explained David.

"He buys and sells between the stallholders and makes himself some money. The regulars know him, and rarely sell to him, but new stallholders are fair game. He doesn't really do any harm as the stallholders are usually happy with their sale and most are none the wiser that their item is being resold at another stall at a higher price. He doubled his money with that book."

It sounded as if David admired Billy's work.

David stopped suddenly beside a stall selling copper and brass jugs, bowls, and plates. He picked up a brass plate, examined it, and returned it to the table. Next, he picked up a copper jug with a delicate spout and a half-moon-shaped top.

As he rotated it, Dotty noticed it was covered in beautiful engravings. He returned the jug to the table, picked up another one, but placed it back on the table before walking away.

Dotty caught up with him and asked, "Did you see anything of interest?"

"Not really," David replied airily. He consulted his leather-strapped watch before turning to Dotty. "I'd like to introduce you to some associates and clients of mine. I'm meeting them in the restaurant."

Dotty and David left the hall and walked past several other sheds until they reached a modern, square, double-height building called The Avon Pavilion.

David entered through glass doors at one corner, and they climbed a flight of stairs to the first floor, arriving at opened onto a seating area with leather sofas and chairs, and at the far end, a coffee bar.

A group of Arab men occupied the sofas and chairs. Two elderly men wore white thawb robes with matching headdresses secured with thick black cords.

When they turned to face them, Dotty thought she recognised one of them. Had he been with David over a year ago at Windrush Hall, when Akemans had auctioned the Duke of Ditchford's possessions?

"As-salamu alaikum," greeted a younger man, wearing a neat grey suit, who jumped to his feet and approached David and Dotty.

David gripped the man's outstretched hand and returned the greeting.

The rest of the men also wore suits.

"Dorothy, this is my friend, Tariq. Tariq, Dorothy, who works with me at Akemans."

"Delighted to meet you." Tariq's large, almond-shaped eyes glinted with amusement.

One of the older men shouted in Arabic and another suited man jumped to his feet and approached the coffee bar.

He returned with a brass tray on which were two handless porcelain cups and an open-topped brass jug with a wooden handle.

Two men rose and offered their chairs to David and Dotty. Not wanting to cause offence, Dotty sat down and accepted the cup of coffee she was handed. She sipped the thick dark liquid, which was strong and bitter. She tried not to grimace.

The two older men started talking to David in Arabic. Feeling self-conscious, Dotty tried to concentrate on her coffee.

Tariq stood in front of her and offered her another cup. "You are an English woman, so I think you prefer tea?"

"Thank you, yes I do." Dotty handed him the handleless cup, which he placed back on the tray before sitting down next to her.

"So you work at Akemans with David. That must be very interesting work."

"Oh, it is," replied Dotty enthusiastically.

"And your area of expertise is?"

Dotty felt the colour rise to her cheeks. "I'm still learning. That's why David brought me here. I think," she added.

As the older men occasionally glanced in her direction, she wondered if there was another reason she'd been invited to the fair. If these men were clients, did he want her to get to know them?

"I like your English countryside. But not in winter. It is too cold." Tariq joked, and she was grateful for his courteous attention. They chatted comfortably for five minutes about English life before David shook the two older men's hands and stood up.

"Thank you," Dotty said to Tariq, as she also stood.

"It was lovely meeting you. I hope to see you again soon."

Dotty wondered where he hoped to see her as she was hardly likely to bump into him at the supermarket in Cirencester, but perhaps David had arranged for him and his colleagues to visit Akemans. She wondered exactly what their business was.

Outside The Avon Pavilion, David asked, "Can you occupy yourself for an hour? I've some work to attend to."

"Of course," replied Dotty, wondering what work David was referring to but, resisting the temptation to follow him, she turned in the opposite direction and entered Hall 5.

The stalls in this hall displayed an assortment of items. She wandered past vintage board games, attractive coloured quilts and throws, and Victorian kitchen items including tarnished copper pans, bone-handled knives and forks, and a large round copper jelly mould.

"Roger, what about the Minton Green tea set?" asked a woman in a nasal voice who was rearranging the display of items at the front of the next stall.

She over enunciated some of her vowels and Dotty thought from her accent that she was from Manchester. The darker strands of her long wavy hair showed beneath the platinum dyed ones and, despite it being January, she wore a cropped white top revealing a flat, tanned tummy and a hanging gold and diamante star-shaped belly button ring.

Pottery, china, and glass ornaments were on display at the stall. The tea set she referred to was at the front with six cups and saucers, a milk jug and sugar bowl.

The woman stallholder picked up the milk jug with her white-gloved hands and placed it beside the teapot.

Each piece was decorated with a pink bird surrounded by pea-green coloured glazing. It wasn't to Dotty's taste. But she did like the threadbare teddy bear sitting on the faded embroidery cushion of a mahogany piano stool in front of the stall.

She picked the teddy bear up as the woman removed her gloves and declared, "£50. £45 for cash."

"Thank you. I'm just looking." Dotty placed the teddy bear back on its stool as a round-faced man, with receding fair hair, called, "Keep the Minton tea set as it is. If we don't sell it this week, I'll reduce the price at the Cotswold Fair. It cost me £150, so I'm loath to let it go for less than £200."

The Cotswold Fair, mused Dotty. That must be nearer to home. She should find out more about it and ask her friend Keya to go with her.

CHAPTER FIVE

Instead of going into her cottage, when she returned from Akemans on Wednesday evening, Dotty entered the adjoining farmhouse and made her way along the terracotta tiled hallway to the kitchen, where she heard a murmur of voices.

Meadowbank Farm, on the edge of the small Cotswold town of Fairford, belonged to Gilly Wimsey and George Carey-Boyd's aunt and uncle.

But Uncle Cliff, who'd farmed it for many years, had developed dementia and although his wife, Aunt Beanie, had tried her best to care for him at home, he'd had an accident just before Christmas and been taken to their local community hospital.

It became clear to all, including Aunt Beanie, that Uncle Cliff could no longer live at home, even though she'd invited Norman Climpson to live in the farmhouse and help look after him.

Norman had worked for the Duke of Ditchford, but when the Duke died, he'd lost his home and his livelihood. He now lived at the farmhouse and worked part time as the porter at Akemans.

Between Christmas and New Year, Uncle Cliff had been moved to a comfortable, but expensive, care home on the edge of another Cotswold town, Burford.

When Dotty entered the warm, welcoming kitchen, heated by a

blue Aga range cooker, she was surprised to find Chief Inspector Ringrose sitting at the rectangular pine kitchen table with Aunt Beanie.

Chief Inspector Ringrose ran Gloucestershire's Rural, Heritage and Wildlife Unit, which Aunt Beanie consulted for. Dotty's police friend, Sergeant Keya Varma, worked in the unit, which was less than a year old.

Norman removed a chrome kettle from a hot plate on the Aga and poured hot water into a teapot.

"You're just in time for tea," proclaimed Aunt Beanie when she saw Dotty.

Dotty looked around, searching for Earl Grey. He normally appeared, or at least acknowledged her from wherever he was sleeping when she appeared.

She moved across to a small hut which Norman had built beside the Aga for Aunt Beanie's pet Berkshire pig, Agatha.

Agatha had been the cause of Uncle Cliff's fall before Christmas and Aunt Beanie had finally accepted that she was too big to live in the kitchen, especially as she and Earl Grey loved playing games and careering about.

Dotty and Aunt Beanie had created a comfortable stall for Agatha in the stone barn outside next to Buttercup, Norman's Jersey cow.

Peering inside the hut, she noted the empty dog basket Agatha had used, even when she'd outgrown it.

Aunt Beanie called, "If you're looking for Earl Grey, he's here on the chief inspector's lap."

Earl Grey rarely showed such favouritism to visitors, normally keeping out of their way.

"You have a fine cat," remarked the chief inspector, who as usual wore a well-cut charcoal-grey suit which covered his slight paunch. He was a distinguished-looking gentleman and from the few times Dotty had met him, she'd assessed he was intelligent, but fair.

"The chief inspector has been telling us all about the ancient clay tablets you and David were called to assess at Cotswold Airport."

Dotty sat down next to the chief inspector. Earl Grey looked at her before nonchalantly licking a paw.

"As David discerned, it is a rare collection dating back to the Ur Dynasty. The British Museum is extremely interested in studying it, although the Iraqi Government has lodged a protest and demanded the collection be returned to them."

Aunt Beanie acknowledged, "That's a tricky one, since you believe it was stolen from their country, but without the Brits, the collection would have been split up and lost forever."

"What was David's opinion of the collection's ownership?" asked Chief Inspector Ringrose. His tone was casual, but Dotty didn't think he'd asked a purely philosophical question.

"He believes that cultural and heritage items belong to their country of origin," Dotty replied.

"And should be returned to them," mused the chief inspector.

"He has a point," claimed Norman, placing cups of tea in front of Dotty and the chief inspector. "And it's not as if we don't have enough artefacts from other countries in our museums, and who knows how many treasures are locked away in storage?"

"Well, it's not our call," declared the chief inspector. "The British Museum is grateful for our … your help, Dorothy, and they will begin to date, examine, and document the tablets in due course."

Chief Inspector Ringrose picked up his cup of tea and added, "And I understand you and Sergeant Varma are visiting the antique fair at Charbury Castle Hotel on Saturday."

"Yes," Dotty confirmed.

"I've told my sergeant that she can count it as a working day."

Dotty grimaced. It wouldn't be much fun wandering around the stalls with Keya in her police uniform.

"But," continued the chief inspector, "she is to wear plain clothes. I don't want her startling the stallholders, many of whom I suspect tread a narrow path between the right and the wrong side of the law."

Norman grunted as he sat down on the far side of the pine table.

The chief inspector looked from him to Aunt Beanie, who sat at the end of the table, and asked, "Will you visit the antique fair?"

"Cliff's care home is having a coffee morning and as new … I was about to say parents, as if Cliff is at school … as new members of the community, Norman and I thought we should support them."

"But not in the financial sense," muttered Norman. "We've been sent our first bill and it's astronomical."

"But you can pay it?" Dotty's voice rose in concern.

Aunt Beanie placed a hand on her arm. "Thanks to the farm, and you and Norman voluntarily increasing your rent payments, we can pay the fees and still live in relative comfort here. Although our needs are quite modest."

"The Land Rover could do with a service, but we aren't buying any flash cars or jetting off to the Caribbean," agreed Norman.

"But depending on when the coffee morning finishes, we might pop over to the antique fair," considered Aunt Beanie.

Norman raised his eyebrows. "I think I'd rather come home. Who knows what'll happen if you, Dotty and Keya get together. But if you do go, Beanie, don't buy any more stuff. We need a clearout here as it is."

CHAPTER SIX

On Saturday morning Dotty picked Keya, Sergeant Varma, up from the modern, Cotswold-stone clad, police station in the centre of Cirencester and drove them both north-east to Charbury Castle Hotel.

As they turned into the drive, lined with ancient oak trees, Dotty thought back to the last time she'd visited the hotel.

She'd been a crew member on *The Antique Tour* which was being filmed at the hotel.

But after an interesting, and at times exciting, day watching members of the public bring their possessions to be valued, one of the antiques experts had been found dead at the bottom of the hotel's grand circular staircase.

Gilmore Chapman had also been an expert that day, and the whole crew had enjoyed supper together in the hotel.

"Are you thinking about the last time you were here?" asked Keya.

"Yes," nodded Dotty.

"It was a sad weekend, but at least we made a new friend."

We did? "Who?" asked Dotty.

"Felix!" exclaimed Keya.

Dotty remembered back to the young man who'd brought a marble bust to be valued just so he could get close to the celebrity antiques expert, as he believed she'd been responsible for damaging his fledgling acting career.

"And we still haven't taken up his offer of free tickets to watch his show in London. He says it's going on tour over the summer, so we must get organised and go."

Dotty smiled. "Oh yes, we must, and we can have supper with …" she was about to say Gilmore, "… with Felix after the show," she added lamely.

She ignored Keya's sideways glance and instead considered the building in front of her. It had a wide stone frontage, topped with square ramparts, broken up by small, mullioned windows, and a large round turret at the right-hand corner.

On her first visit, David had told her about its colourful history. Built in early Tudor times, it became a royal palace and there was a story that Henry VIII had stayed with his new Queen, Anne Boleyn, after their secret marriage.

Unfortunately, the main part of the castle burnt down during the nineteenth century and was left in ruins until a rich London financier rebuilt it as a family home.

In the 1950s, it was converted into a hotel and, more recently, refurbished to provide luxury accommodation. There was also a spa which David said his wife, Marion, liked to visit with friends.

As it was winter, and too wet to park in the field which had been used for *The Antiques Tour*, they found a space on the drive's wide grass verge, but Dotty was careful to keep two wheels on the tarmac. She didn't want to get stuck.

The heavy snow which had fallen on Christmas Day had stayed until new year. Although the temperature had risen, ominous black clouds moved slowly and laboriously across the sky and it looked likely to rain at some point during the day.

Dotty pulled her blue padded jacket closed and zipped it up snuggly. She and Keya walked towards the hotel, noticing the marquees spreading out to the left of the building, and entered through the revolving front doors.

Dotty glanced up the central staircase to the glass domed roof as a female voice asked, "Are you here for the fair?"

"Yes," confirmed Keya.

"That'll be £5 each admission fee, which includes a list of the stallholders."

Keya handed over a £10 note and asked, "Can I have a receipt, please?"

"Of course."

As the young woman wrote out the receipt, Keya confided, "If I'm on duty, I may as well claim the entrance cost."

"But I'm not police," Dotty protested.

"You're part of my cover, and a subject matter expert."

The young woman handed Keya a receipt and two sheets of paper as she explained, "The bar is open for hot and cold drinks, and meals are being served in our restaurant throughout the day."

Keya handed Dotty a list of stallholders and asked, "Where shall we start?"

"Let's begin with the stalls in here, and then work our way outside."

The area to the right of the reception usually had comfortable armchairs and sofas, but they'd been removed to make way for stalls selling jewellery and smaller items of gold and silver.

"I don't need any more jewellery." Keya shook her wrist to highlight the silver bangle she wore. "And I see you are wearing Jay's snowflake necklace and earrings."

Dotty touched the delicate silver snowflake hanging around her neck. Jay Newton, a former rock star, local celebrity, and friend, had given her and Keya the jewellery they were wearing as Christmas presents.

"Oh, but look at this ruby ring. The stone's huge." Keya knelt down by the glass front of one of the stalls to examine the ring. "Wow, it's label says £3,500."

"I'm sure the owner would barter the price down," suggested Dotty.

"Not low enough," joked her friend. As she straightened up, she knocked an adjacent glass cabinet, which rocked and a small silver pheasant fell off. "Oh toda!"

Dotty jumped forward and caught the ornament before it hit the red-carpeted floor.

"Thank you," gasped her friend. "That could have been expensive."

Dotty replaced the pheasant on the stall and they moved on, examining a display of beautifully engraved teaspoons, a collection of silver thimbles, and a cushion displaying earrings with precious and semi-precious stones.

At one stall, a woman held a small u-shaped magnet up against a silver gravy boat. The woman sighed as the gravy boat was attracted to the magnet and she returned it to the stall.

"What was that all about?" asked Keya.

"Real silver is not noticeably magnetic, but fake silver and silver-plated items are often made from metals which are. I guess that lady was looking for an item of pure silver."

"Let's grab a hot drink," suggested Keya. "I need a break before examining any more stalls."

Dotty and Keya passed through the reception area and Dotty thought she spotted David disappearing outside via the revolving doors.

The bar area was busy, but a family of four moved away from a table as they appeared.

"I'll buy the drinks since you paid our entrance fee," insisted Dotty.

"The unit paid our entrance fee, but I'm not going to argue. A cappuccino, please," Keya requested as she sat on a stool at the empty table.

Dotty collected Keya's coffee and her tea from the counter but as she returned to their table she noted, with amusement, that Ethel and Edith, the two old ladies David had pointed out at the Bath Antique Fair, had sat down at Keya's table.

They both wore yellow jumpers and seemed to be ignoring her friend as they animatedly discussed a ruby ring.

As Dotty sat down, she heard the one with straight white hair remark, "You don't see rubies that size or clarity in rings very often. The last time I did was at a fair in Worcester, and it sold for well over £5,000."

Dotty grinned as she placed the two cups she was carrying on the table and sat down. She winked at Keya and leaned towards the elderly women.

"Hello ladies, it's Ethel and Edith, isn't it? I'm Dotty, from Akemans, and this is my friend, Sergeant Varma."

The two women gulped. The one with curly hair stuttered, "Lovely to meet you, my dear. But we can't hang around chatting, can we, Ethel?"

Both women jumped to their feet and dashed away.

"I think you've forgotten something," called Dotty after them.

She held up their aluminium walking sticks, which they snatched from her, before making a less speedy exit.

CHAPTER SEVEN

"So tell me again," insisted Keya, "Who were those two old ladies and why did they make such a hasty escape when you introduced us?"

Dotty grinned, as she peeled off her jacket, and said, "David Rook pointed them out at the Bath Antique Fair. They're called Ethel and Edith and I don't think they're nearly as frail as they make out."

"They certainly didn't need their walking sticks when they hurried away."

"It's probably all part of their act. David says they make a deal with a stallholder on the price of a particular object, and if they introduce a buyer who pays above that amount, they're paid the difference."

Keya wrinkled her forehead. "And how do they do that?"

"Persuade a buyer to pay over the odds, with tactics like the ones they were trying to use on you. They make a person feel they are missing out on an expensive or rare item, so they have to have it."

"FOMO," Keya remarked.

"What?"

"Fear of missing out. Society seems obsessed with it at the moment. And it's leading to jealousy and crime. I see it all the time with my work. A family sees another family on social media having a wonderful time on an expensive holiday and feels they need a holiday as well.

"So they steal or do something stupid to get the money. What they don't see is the huge loan the first family took out, or the continual rows the parents had when they were away. People only post the happy moments. It's not reality."

"I guess that's why I'm not one for social media. And my friends live near me, and I like talking to them face-to-face," conceded Dotty.

"So the old biddies make other people think they're missing out on an opportunity, and human nature being what it is, the person buys the item and doesn't care that they're paying too much for it," Keya concluded.

"Very neatly put."

"I can't actually see they're committing a crime, although it isn't exactly honest."

Dotty and Keya sipped their drinks.

At the neighbouring table a woman said, "So this is what your Roger does every weekend? Hang out with the well-to-do in luxury hotels?"

A woman in her fifties with long, wavy, blonde hair, which looked too light to be natural, and bright-pink painted nails, replied, "I don't think these fairs are always in hotels. Last weekend he was at the Bath Showground, which isn't exactly glamorous."

"Doesn't he get bored?" a third woman asked.

"To be honest, if it keeps him out of trouble and out of my hair, I'm happy. It means I can go on weekend hikes. And he makes a few bob. There was no work for him around us once the factory closed down.

"He started buying lost property from British Rail and selling it at car boot sales. Now he buys at car boot sales, and at auctions and house clearances. As I said, he's not under my feet and he's making his own beer money. The salon pays the household bills."

"Well, I think you've very tolerant," responded the first woman.

"And trusting," added the third.

As the three women pushed back their stools, one of them asked the lady with long, wavy, blonde hair, "Did Roger give you that diamond brooch?"

"He did, one of the few romantic gestures he's made. He said the star is the symbol of truth and honesty."

They left the bar.

"Finished?" asked Keya.

"Oh. Yes," replied Dotty.

Keya cleared away their cups, and they walked out of the bar by the side door and across the tarmac drive, which ran round the side of the hotel, towards the first marquee.

"I'm glad you told me to bring a jacket," admitted Keya, as they both pulled on their coats. "It's already spitting with rain."

Inside the marquee, Dotty spotted the three ladies from the bar at a stall. It was one she'd seen at the Bath Antique Fair, which mostly displayed pottery, china and glass ornaments.

The tea set with the pink bird and pea-green decoration was still on the stall, and as they drew closer, she noted the price was £150. She was sure the stallholder said he'd bought it for that amount, so he wouldn't make any profit.

Dotty's musing was disturbed when one of the women screamed, "And who are you, you …" Dotty winced at the next word.

"I could ask you the same thing!" shouted back the gum-chewing stallholder with the Mancunian accent and the pierced belly button. "Flouncing up to this stall and making comments as if you own it."

The woman from the bar with long, wavy, blonde hair planted her hands on her hips and called the younger woman some obscene names.

Finally she added, "And I do, or at least my good for nothing husband does. Where's Roger?"

"That's what I want to know," yelled back the gum-chewing woman from behind her stall.

"There he is!" shouted another of the women from the bar.

They all turned as a plump man with fair hair disappeared out of the marquee towards the hotel.

The two women who'd been arguing ran after him.

Dotty realised everyone in the marquee had stopped to watch the altercation.

They now started whispering to each other, as one of the remaining two women from the bar turned to her friend and said, "No wonder Roger was so keen to get away from Natalie and go to antique fairs every weekend. He had a younger bit on the side."

CHAPTER EIGHT

Ethel and Edith peeled themselves away from a stall on the opposite side of the marquee.

Along with their light yellow jumpers, Edith, with the curly hair, wore similarly coloured trousers and Ethel, with straight white hair, wore a cream skirt decorated with yellow flowers.

As they passed Dotty and Keya, Dotty heard Edith quip, "It serves Roger right. Threatening to tell punters that Edith and Ethel are not nice old ladies."

"And all because he refused to pay us £800. We agreed on a price for that Murano glass vase, fair and square. He was the one who cheated us," Ethel responded in an affronted tone.

Keya turned to Dotty. "I thought an antique fair would be civilised and uneventful, but I'm already starting to enjoy myself. There are plenty of colourful characters."

Dotty didn't think she only meant the yellow-clad Ethel and Edith, who already appeared to be in discussion with another stallholder about a clock.

Dotty and Keya continued to browse the stalls in the marquee.

"Let's look at those on the right-hand side now and, when we come back, we can see those on the left?" suggested Keya.

The first marquee opened into a second one, with similar stalls to the first, and they continued through it, stopping every now and again to examine a trinket, bowl, or other interesting item.

Keya stopped at a stall displaying baking equipment and cake and tarts tins, including the standard round and square ones, but also stars, shells, and other novelty shapes.

"Some of these might be useful for my afternoon tea course next week," considered Keya.

"I didn't know you were doing that. It sounds fun. What will you do?"

"We start with a history of afternoon tea and then we get into the baking. I'm happy with the sweet things, like scones and cakes, but I'm not sure they'll have many vegetarian options for the savoury side."

"I bet they do, and vegan and other options for different food allergies," Dotty surmised.

Keya looked up, holding a metal madeleine tray with twelve shell-shaped indents, and added in an excited voice. "At the end of the week there's a session on teas, and another about preparing the table and serving guests."

She bit her lip before adding, "And we can ask two guests to join us on Friday afternoon. I wondered if you and Aunt Beanie would come?"

"I'd love to, and I can't see Aunt Beanie turning down a free tea. Where is it?"

"Hilcot Manor, about ten miles north of Cirencester."

"As long as I can get the time off work, I'll be there. And that's a nice baking tray. It hardly looks used. Madeleines aren't too difficult as long as you don't overcook them. I add a touch of lemon zest to mine."

"Should I buy it?" asked Keya nervously.

"Why not? If you smile and engage with the stallholder, she'll be more likely to haggle with you, and if you think it's too expensive, just walk away. Do you have cash to pay for it?"

Keya nodded as she lifted up the madeleine tray and caught the stallholders' eye. "Hi. How much is this?" she asked.

"£10," the lady replied.

Keya's shoulders slumped. "That's quite a lot when I don't know how much I'm going to use it. I'm going on a baking course next week, you see."

"Good for you," replied the stallholder. "Too many people don't bother making cakes these days, and just buy from supermarkets. I tell you what, I'll throw in this set of six fluted mini-French patisserie tins as well. They're really useful for individual quiches or tarts."

"OK," agreed Keya, and handed over a ten-pound note. The lady wrapped her purchases in newspaper and placed them in a brown paper bag, which she passed to Keya.

Keya stuffed the bag into a bright patchwork sling bag which she was carrying over her shoulder.

The third and final marquee had fewer stalls, which were spread out and selling larger items. Keya approached one selling vintage furniture and paintings.

She pointed to a portrait of a man in an ornate gilt frame, who had a grey beard and wore a sombre black jacket. "He doesn't look like much fun, does he?"

"I wouldn't want him staring down at me from my living room wall," agreed Dotty. "But I do like the small oak table next to him. And the large Union Jack flag hanging at the back."

But neither item perked her interest enough to enquire about their prices.

"I think this is the last one," commented Keya as they glanced across at a stall selling vintage bicycles and domed glass display cases, which Dotty could imagine once covered stuffed owls or other birds.

"Shall we make our way back? Is there anything in particular you're looking for?" asked Keya.

"Not really, although there was a pair of pretty serving bowls with roses on them which I quite liked, but I don't really do any entertaining now. I usually join Aunt Beanie in the farmhouse."

"I bet she has enough stuff to run her own stall at one of these events," considered Keya.

"You're probably right. But I'm not sure where she'd start. Every cupboard and corner in the farmhouse is crammed full."

They both grinned as they turned and retraced their steps. From this angle, they noticed new items even on stalls they had previously looked at, and pointed at them with interest.

"What's this?" asked Keya, as she patted the head of a metal horse the size of a large dog. "It doesn't look like a rocking horse."

The stallholder, a smiling woman in her mid-forties, explained, "Children can ride it. They push up and down on the metal bar of the stirrups and the horse moves forward."

"That sounds like fun," laughed Keya.

"And it's in excellent condition," added the stallholder.

"I don't have kids, but thanks," replied Keya.

As they wandered on, Dotty asked, "Do you want children? I think I've asked you before, but I wondered if you feel differently now your younger sister's getting married?"

Keya considered a pair of long-handled toasting forks, one with a heart-shaped end and one with a star.

She picked up the one with the star-shaped end as she replied, "I'm not sure. I've always been independent, and while I love and respect my family, I don't believe that what they consider best for us all is always right for me."

She put the toasting fork down, but continued to stare at it. "They were horrified when I went off on my own and joined the police force."

She looked up at Dotty. "I don't think my mum has forgiven me. I'm the oldest and she's desperate for grandchildren. And now, no self-respecting Hindu man that meets my parents' approval would marry a police officer."

Dotty touched the cold metal barrel of a toy cannon. "But what about a husband of your own choosing? Do you need your parents' approval?"

They moved on to the next stall. "No, I suppose not. But I'm caught in the middle. Non-Hindu boys presume I'm out of bounds and there isn't exactly a lot of choice in Cirencester police station."

"What about Sergeant Unwin?" asked Dotty. "You two have been working closely together lately."

Keya looked at Dotty, her eyebrows drawn together. "His interests lie elsewhere."

Dotty was uncertain how to respond.

"The trouble is," confessed Keya, "that although I chose to be a police officer over my family, I'm not sure I want to be one forever. But I can't see myself as a stay-at-home wife with three or four children either."

"I thought you enjoyed your work, especially those parts involving the community. And you've done a fantastic job organising charity events."

"Except that people die at them," replied Keya in a flat tone. Keya had organised a charity team triathlon in the summer, where one of the competitors had died, and a guest was killed at the recent Christmas charity ball she and Dotty had organised.

Dotty offered Keya a sad smile. "That's not your fault."

"I know, but Jay wants me to organise an upmarket tabletop or car boot sale at Windrush Hall. What if I'm jinxed and someone else dies?"

"I'm sure they won't." Dotty linked her arm through Keya's and they wandered along in front of stalls selling vintage children's toys and dolls.

As they re-entered the first marquee, Dotty glanced towards the stall where the earlier altercation had been.

"No way, they're arguing again," exclaimed Keya, following Dotty's gaze.

"The man on the stall, Roger is," agreed Dotty, "but I'm not sure whether that's his wife or girlfriend."

"I think his girlfriend was wearing jeans, so it's probably his wife, furious at finding out about his girlfriend. Never a dull moment," conceded Keya.

They stopped beside a bookstall.

"These are a bit highbrow for me," complained Keya. "All about philosophy," she picked up a black-bound book with a man's face on the front, "and politics from twenty years ago." She quickly replaced it.

Dotty had found an interesting collection of hardback books about antiques and collecting on a wooden shelf.

She pulled one out which specialised in Hallmarks on British gold and silver, and replied, "You remember Aunt Beanie gave Norman Victor Frankl's book, Man's Search for Meaning, for Christmas?"

"Yes," replied Keya, "It also looked a difficult read. I prefer a steamy romance."

"You don't?"

Keya bowed her head and muttered. "Occasionally."

Dotty laughed. "Well, Norman has really got into his book. He said he didn't have the opportunity for a good education, and is fascinated by it. He keeps wanting to discuss his true purpose in life."

Dotty picked up a book on investing in pottery and porcelain and, holding it up with the one about silver hallmarks, asked the stallholder. "How much?"

"£10."

Dotty hesitated.

"And I'll throw in this one about Babylonian Antiquities."

"OK." Dotty handed over a ten-pound note and took the third book from the stallholder.

"Who wants to read about old relics?" dismissed Keya. "I bet the seller's delighted to get rid of that book."

"You never know when it might come in useful," countered Dotty.

As they approached the stall where the two women had been arguing earlier, they saw a young man with short, dark, slightly wispy hair talking to Roger, the overweight stallholder.

"Billy, I'm not buying." Roger shook his head at the younger man, who Dotty recognised from the Bath Antique Fair.

She caught Keya's arm and pulled her to a stop as she whispered, "That man, Billy, makes a living buying from one stall and selling to another at a higher price, but I don't think Roger is interested."

Roger said, "No. Not after you bought that Rudolf Schrotter vase from me last week. I know you sold it to Sid. He's selling it on his stall for £800, yet you swore it was a fake. You'll not play games with me, pal. I'll not be made a fool of."

Keya nudged Dotty. "Come on, I'm starving. Let's find something to eat."

CHAPTER NINE

Dotty and Keya re-entered Charbury Castle Hotel.

"I don't feel like a large lunch, and the restaurant here is expensive," Dotty said.

"What about that?" Keya pointed to a sign in the reception area.

They approached it and Keya read, "Light lunches and snacks are being served in The Orangery. What's that?"

"I think it's like a conservatory, but I don't know where it is," replied Dotty.

The smiling receptionist from earlier approached them and asked, "Would you like directions to The Orangery?"

"Yes, please," Dotty replied.

"Go out of the side door by the restaurant, across the drive and along a short gravel path. The Orangery is the old greenhouse which we renovated this summer and turned into a tearoom. It isn't usually open in the winter, but there are so many people today, the bar and restaurant can't cope, so we've opened it up."

Dotty and Keya followed the receptionist's directions and arrived at a building which was part miniature castle, complete with a turret, and part old-fashioned glass house.

They walked through the entrance turret and entered the glasshouse. The building had a stone frame, matching the castle theme, with large, arch-shaped mullion windows along each side and a series of pointed pyramidal glass roof sections.

Wide double doors led onto an outdoor stone patio area at the front, but they were currently closed.

The Orangery was half full, and they easily found a table by a window, although it was set for four people.

As they sat down, Dotty mused wistfully, "I wonder what exotic blooms were once nurtured in here."

Dotty's thoughts were drawn back to the present as a figure rushed past the window wearing a grey jacket or jumper with something pink printed on the back.

"I bet they only grew vegetables," replied Keya. "It looks more like a … what's the word for a useless old building rich people built?"

"I think you mean a folly, although this building did have a practical purpose."

"But it didn't need a turret. What some people spend their money on." Keya shook her head. She picked up the menu and winced. "And they're not the only ones. £6.00 for a sandwich and £7.50 for a filled panini."

"They are served with crisps, coleslaw and a side salad," Dotty pointed out.

"Which will cost about 50p. This cafe business is a licence to print money."

"Not exactly," countered Dotty, who'd run a small cafe on the first floor of Akemans Antiques centre leading up to Christmas. But she'd been giving away hot drinks, mince pies and Christmas fruit cake to customers of the antiques centre, and she hadn't paid any rent.

"There are food costs, and the wastage. Fresh food has a short shelf life. And you need to pay staff."

Keya sat back. "I've always liked the idea of a small deli and cafe in a quaint Cotswold village."

"I don't think it'll be as idyllic as you make out, and you'll need to attract locals in the winter to supplement the summer tourists. But don't worry about lunch. I'll buy."

"Are you sure?" asked Keya sheepishly.

"As long as you don't order the seafood platter."

Dotty and Keya studied the menu and discussed some of the items they'd seen on the stalls.

"Can I take your order?" asked a waitress dressed all in black.

"A coronation chicken baguette, please," replied Dotty

"Cranberry and brie toastie, please," Keya said.

Two of the women who'd been in the bar earlier entered The Orangery and looked around.

"I thought Natalie might be in here," remarked one of them, who had straight dark hair and was wearing a red blouse with a black jacket and trousers. She also wore a pair of red high-heel shoes.

The second lady, with a fuller figure, who wore a navy chiffon maxi dress with a brown suede jacket and matching boots, replied, "I thought so too, since she wasn't in the restaurant, but I'm not waiting for her."

Keya leaned towards Dotty and whispered, "Isn't Natalie the one who had a row with the woman on the stall? And aren't those two her friends, who sat near us in the bar?"

"Yes, I wonder what's happened to Natalie?"

"She's probably gone home and is currently packing her husband's things and throwing them out of the window into the garden. That's what I'd do if I found out my husband was cheating on me."

Natalie's friends must have had similar thoughts as the one with the red high heels, who'd crossed one leg elegantly over the other, considered, "How are we going to get home if Natalie has already left?"

A waitress appeared and placed Dotty's and Keya's sandwiches on the table. She returned with a teapot and cup for Dotty and a cappuccino for Keya.

"I need the caffeine to wake me up. I didn't realise looking around antique stalls would be so tiring," confessed Keya.

The Orangery had filled up and as Dotty was about to bite into her sandwich, she heard a cough and looked up.

"I'm sorry to bother you," said a man in his mid-thirties, whose shirt was unbuttoned one too many holes, revealing a thick mat of dark chest hair. "Can I join you? All the tables are full."

"Of course." Keya gave the man a huge, inviting smile.

Dotty was surprised her friend didn't bat her eyelashes at the newcomer, and she looked down to hide a giggle.

"Don't let me stop you eating your lunch," the man said. "I'm Quinn, by the way."

"Keya," said Keya, reaching forward with her hand, "And this is Dotty," she added as Quinn shook her hand.

Quinn hailed a passing waitress and asked, "Can I have a cappuccino and a chicken and bacon panini, toasted." As the waitress left, he looked down at the spare chair on which Dotty had placed her books. "You're a collector, are you?"

"Not me," blurted Keya, before Dotty, had a chance to reply. "Those are Dotty's. She works at Akemans?"

"Akemans?"

"A local auction house and antiques centre?"

"I'm not from around here. I'm staying with my parents. They've had a few issues which I'm trying to sort out."

Just then, the yellow-clad Ethel and Edith entered The Orangery. Two men sitting close to Dotty's table hailed them and they hurried across.

"You look excited," one of the men said. "Have you fleeced another punter?"

"We don't fleece people," replied Edith indignantly.

"Just persuade them," replied Ethel. "Anyway, that's not it. It's Roger Dewhirst."

Quinn's hand shook, and he spilt his cappuccino.

Ethel and Edith chorused in unison. "He's dead."

CHAPTER TEN

It was as if the occupants of The Orangery had entered suspended animation. Cups stopped halfway up to people's lips and forks remained in customers' mouths. All chatter ceased instantly.

"Say that again," requested the man sitting at the table beside Ethel and Edith.

Ethel flattened her white hair with her hand and looked around her mesmerised audience, before announcing, "Roger Dewhirst has been found dead behind his stall, with a large toasting fork sticking out of his chest."

Keya gulped.

Quinn placed his cup on its saucer. His hand was still shaking and liquid slopped over the side. "No way," he muttered.

Other customers began moving and chattering excitedly.

Before Dotty had time to ask Quinn if he knew the deceased, Natalie entered the conservatory. She ran a pink-nailed hand through her long, wavy, blonde hair as she looked around.

Oblivious to the other customers' stares, she spotted her two friends and strolled across to their table.

"Sorry, I'm late. I was so furious with Roger that I jumped straight in the car, but half-way home I thought, why should I let him ruin my day? And drove back. What's the matter?"

Natalie's two well-dressed friends both gawped at her open-mouthed.

Finally, the one wearing the red heels stammered, "Haven't you heard? Roger's dead."

"Don't be ridiculous. I saw him not long ago ..." she faltered, and then continued, "We all did, and he was alive and well. Although when I get my hands on him ..."

Keya pushed back her chair and jumped to her feet, knocking against the table. More of Quinn's cappuccino sloshed over the side of his cup.

"Excuse me," Keya interrupted, "I'm a police officer."

Dotty heard a shriek. She thought it came from Ethel or Edith.

The colour drained from Quinn's face.

"Perhaps you could come with me, Mrs Dewhirst?"

"It's Mrs Wright," responded Natalie, in what sounded like an automated response. "I didn't take Roger's name when we married. I had my salon to think about."

"Mrs Wright. Please come with me while we establish what has happened."

Natalie turned on her black-heeled boots and led Keya out of The Orangery.

"Excuse me," whispered Dotty to Quinn, pushing back her chair. She chased after her friend.

Dotty heard sirens as she hurried along the gravel path and instead of re-entering the hotel, she followed the drive around to the front.

A police car with flashing lights was racing down the drive as a yellow and green ambulance turned into the entrance. There was no sign of Keya or Natalie.

She heard the hum of an engine idling behind her as she watched the ambulance approach the hotel. As soon as it stopped, a vintage silver Mercedes swept past her and she caught a glimpse of dark hair. Was that David speeding away from the fair?

Two ambulance crew wearing moss-green uniforms entered the revolving doors of the hotel as Dotty walked calmly past them and turned towards the white marquees of the antique fair.

As she was about to enter the first marquee, she glanced back and saw Sergeant Unwin's metallic grey Mercedes sweep down the drive. She ducked inside.

"Ladies and gentlemen, please keep your distance. This is a crime scene," announced Keya, holding her hands up and addressing a small crowd who'd gathered in front of Roger's stall. She saw Dotty and signalled for her to come over.

As Dotty did so, Keya whispered in a desperate tone. "Apparently uniform are on their way, but can you keep these people at bay until they arrive? I need to deal with Mrs Dewhirst … I mean Wright. She won't stop staring at the body. It's rather morbid."

"So he is dead?" whispered Dotty.

Keya turned her back to the crowd and muttered, "Yes, and just as those two old biddies said, a long-handled fork is poking out of his chest … and it looks just like the one I picked up earlier."

"Sergeant Varma," called a uniformed female police officer.

Dotty melted away and ducked round the side of the stall next to Roger's. Conveniently, it had two ladder stands displaying linen and quilts between it and Roger's stall.

Dotty hid behind them and peered through gaps in the rungs, observing the area behind Roger's stall.

Keya was comforting a crying Natalie, who was staring down at her husband. Roger was flat on his back with the three large prongs of a long-handled metal toasting fork sticking out of his chest.

The end of the fork had a star shape and, as Keya had observed, looked exactly like the one she'd picked up at a stall in the second marquee.

How had someone sneaked up on Roger and stabbed him with such a weapon in a marquee full of people?

"That's enough, ladies and gentlemen," bellowed a deep baritone Welsh voice. It was Inspector Evans from Cirencester police station.

"Please make your way down to the end of the marquee, where uniformed officers will take your contact details, and any information you can give them about the deceased and his death."

The crowd surrounding Roger's stall moved steadily down the marquee, shepherded by the uniformed policewoman.

Glancing back behind Roger's stall, Dotty watched Sergeant Evans, in his habitual brown suit, which clung to his stocky body, approach Keya.

"Looks like another fine mess you've got us into," the Inspector remarked without humour.

"I think," responded Sergeant Unwin, stepping into Dotty's line of vision, "that this is a relative of the deceased."

Sergeant Unwin must have been playing sport when he was called to investigate the death, as he was dressed in a pair of black shorts, a grey T-shirt and white trainers.

The inspector turned to Natalie and said, "Beg your pardon, Mrs?"

"Wright," sobbed Natalie.

"And is the deceased your husband, Mr Wright?"

"Yes," Natalie sobbed again. "I mean no."

The inspector pulled at his fleshy chin. "Is he, or isn't he?"

"Inspector," interjected Keya, "The deceased is Roger, Mrs Wright's husband. But his surname is Dewhirst."

Inspector Evans turned to Sergeant Unwin and queried, "Have you got that Sergeant Onion?"

The sergeant winced.

Dotty wondered when the inspector would get his name right.

"The deceased is Roger Dewhirst, and his wife is?" asked the inspector.

"Natalie Wright," confirmed Keya.

"Thank you, Sergeant Varma." Inspector Evans sniffed the air and looked around.

Dotty ducked behind the ladder stands.

"And wherever you are, that meddling friend of yours will be," reasoned the inspector. He called, "Miss Sayers, come out and tell us what you can about the murder weapon." He knew she was called Mrs Sayers.

As Dotty stepped out from behind the ladder stands, she caught Sergeant Unwin's amused smile, before Inspector Evans directed, "Sergeant Unwin, please take Mrs Wright's statement. Sergeant Varma, stay with me."

Sergeant Unwin led Natalie away as Dotty stepped round an old-fashioned galvanised zinc washing barrel containing a wooden washing dolly which looked like a four-legged stool with a long handle, and a copper plunger.

"What can you tell me about the murder weapon?" asked the inspector.

"That Keya, Sergeant Varma, was one of the last people to touch it. It was one of a pair displayed on a stall in the middle marquee. It might be worth seeing if the second one is still there."

"So you've seen this before, Sergeant?"

"Yes sir. I'm not sure why I picked it up. Out of curiosity about its weight I guess."

"Was it heavy?"

"Not as heavy as it looks."

"As your friend suggested, can you see if the other one is still on display?" asked the inspector.

As Dotty and Inspector Evans waited for Keya to return, the inspector asked, "Did you know the deceased?"

Dotty shook her head. "But I think he was a regular at these fairs. We overheard his wife say as much, and I saw him last week at one at Bath Showground."

Keya joined them, panting, and held up a transparent evidence bag. "Here it is."

"This one has a heart-shaped-end," observed Inspector Evans, "whereas the one used as the murder weapon has a star-shaped end. I wonder if that is significant?"

"I think," concluded Keya, "that we can rule out a crime of passion. Surely an irate wife or lover would have stabbed him with the heart-shaped one."

CHAPTER ELEVEN

"Choosing a weapon with a star on it rather than a heart does not rule out the deceased's wife," declared Inspector Evans.

"And as she is my number one suspect, I should find her and my young sergeant and interview her. Are you on or off duty today, Sergeant Varma? I never can tell." The inspector wrinkled his forehead.

"On duty. But more as a study day," replied Keya.

"Hmm. Well, why don't you and your friend study the people in the hotel, and the rest of the antique fair? And listen out for anyone with a grudge against the deceased or a reason to want him out of the way. I'll ask one of the constables to search the stall, but I doubt we'll find anything of use. People will have been coming and going all day and messed about with things."

Inspector Evans turned away towards the marquee entrance and nodded at the two uniformed ambulance personnel.

As the ambulance team approached and squatted beside the body, Keya and Dotty moved round to the front of the stall where a tall, young police constable, wearing blue latex gloves, began his search.

As they watched him, Keya commented, "Rather him than me, with all that glass around. I'd be bound to break something expensive."

The constable picked up a purple glass bowl filled with scraps of paper and considered the contents before placing it back on the table.

Keya stepped towards him and advised, "You better bag those. They might be someone's unwanted shopping list, or the remains of a threatening note. But good luck piecing them back together in the station."

The constable reddened as he tipped the pieces of paper into a transparent evidence bag.

"We can't stand around here all afternoon," Dotty declared. "We need to start investigating. And as the inspector and Sergeant Unwin are with Natalie, Roger's wife, why don't we find his girlfriend?"

"I haven't seen her since she and Natalie shouted at each other," admitted Keya.

Dotty moved towards the bottom end of the marquee, where the crowd was smaller. She realised that once people had given their details to the female police constable, they were being directed through to the middle marquee.

She also noted that the other stalls in this marquee were no longer manned. It wouldn't be a good business day for their owners, but at least it would be better than Roger Dewhirst's day had been.

"She's not in here," Dotty said as she turned back to Keya. "Let's look in the hotel."

Outside, they spotted more police cars and a constable standing beside the entrance to the marquee. He was explaining to two middle-aged women, "I'm afraid you can't come in here, but there is an entrance further down."

At least the other stallholders could continue to trade.

Dotty and Keya entered the hotel by the side door into the bar, which was packed with people, all chatting loudly.

"Let's look in here first," called Dotty, above the noise.

They pushed and shoved their way past men and women who were either standing or seated at tables.

Dotty caught snippets of conversation, which generally included the words 'Roger' and 'dead'. Taking a breath, she squeezed between two particularly tall men and reached the bar area, which was quieter than the rest of the room.

With wide eyes, Keya inclined her head towards a woman seated at the bar with platinum blonde hair covering darker strands beneath. She mouthed, "Is that the girlfriend?"

Dotty strode forward and leaned against the bar.

"What would you like?" asked the barman.

"Two orange juices and lemonades, please," was the first drink that came to Dotty's mind.

Turning to the seated woman, she added, "It's hot in here, isn't it?"

The woman wiped an eye and muttered, "I suppose so."

Uncertain how to further engage the woman, Dotty was relieved when Keya held up her warrant card and said, "I'm Sergeant Varma from Gloucestershire Police and I'd like to ask you some questions."

The woman gulped, swivelled around on her barstool to face Keya, and replied, "About Roger?"

Dotty noticed dried blood on the woman's tummy, and her star-shaped belly button ring was missing.

Keya rummaged in her patchwork sling bag and removed a notebook.

As Dotty sat down, Keya asked the woman, "Can you tell me your name, date of birth, address and telephone number?"

"Keely Clarke. Two e's and one l in Keely, and Clarke with an e."

Dotty worked out from Keely's date of birth that she was thirty-seven and learned that she lived in Bristol, although from her nasal voice and over enunciated vowels, she still thought Keely originated from Manchester.

"And you are here today …?" enquired Keya.

"I always help Roger out at weekends. I work from home during the week, so I enjoy visiting posh places like this. And Roger and I have fun, if you know what I mean? He always took me to a smart restaurant on a Saturday night, although he preferred renting an apartment rather than staying in a hotel. He said it was more private."

Keely giggled. "We liked to have a little excitement."

Dotty felt her face redden, but Keya didn't miss a beat. It must be all the steamy romance novels she read.

"I'm sure you did," remarked Keya. "A young, attractive woman like yourself. But what about his wife?" Keya wasn't pulling her punches today.

Keely winced. "Lying toad. He admitted he had a wife but said she was in a wheelchair, and he had to look after her all week. Told me she either went to a centre or he got in help over the weekend while he attended the fairs. And they were his only release."

"Was today the first time you'd met his wife? If so, it must have been a shock?" Keya suggested.

"You're telling me! I was not expecting a well-groomed and, well …, mobile woman." Keely indicated to the barman and ordered, "Vodka and coke. Double. Go easy on the coke."

Turning back to Keya, she added, "But she has a mouth on her. I haven't heard language like that since I was back in Manchester."

Dotty had been right about the accent.

"We both ran after Roger, but, well, I went and hid in the toilets."

Dotty could see Keely was genuinely upset and wondered what it must be like to share your life with a man you discovered had been lying to you all along.

Still, Roger had admitted he was married, but he'd probably given her a sob story about being lonely, and a slave to his wife when, in reality, his wife seemed to have given him a lot of leeway.

"So when did you find out Roger was dead?" asked Keya, continuing to act professionally.

The barman placed a tumbler in front of Keely, and she picked it up and downed half the black, bubbly liquid. Wiping her lips, she explained, "Eventually, I composed myself enough to go back to the stall and grab my stuff, but when I was about to enter the marquee, someone rushed out shouting about a dead man inside. I just knew it was Roger."

"Why?" asked Dotty, intrigued.

"Things had been going wrong all day. It wasn't just the miraculous recovery and appearance of his wife, there were people threatening him. Those two old biddies, Ethel and Edith, claimed he owed them money, and a man accused him of swindling his parents. It just wasn't Roger's day."

"But you didn't expect him to die?" questioned Dotty.

"Not unless it was a heart attack. He didn't have a particularly healthy lifestyle, so I could have understood that." Keely downed the rest of her drink.

CHAPTER TWELVE

Keely Clarke slammed her glass down on the bar at Charbury Castle Hotel and lifted her arm to catch the barman's attention.

"I think you've had enough for the moment," Keya cautioned. "Inspector Evans will want to speak to you."

"Who?" and as the barman approached, Keely slurred, "Same again."

He looked up at Keya, who shook her head and instructed, "You better come with us, Miss Clarke."

"Get off me," cried Keely as Keya took hold of her arm.

Dotty was impressed by Keya's professionalism, as she remained composed and stated, "Either you can come with me calmly and willingly, or I'll fetch a couple of constables who'll handcuff you if necessary."

"What? I haven't done anything."

Those people sitting and standing closet to the bar stopped talking and watched the three women warily.

Dotty leaned towards Keely and asked, "Don't you want to know what happened to Roger?"

"Not really," sniffed Keely, as her lips and chin trembled.

"I do think you should come with us. How are you getting home this evening? Do you have a car?" asked Dotty in a gentle voice.

Keely sniffed again. "It's in the village, at the place we're staying." She sobbed and corrected herself. "The place we were staying at."

Keya placed her hand on Keely's arm again and this time Keely slid off her barstool and allowed herself to be escorted away from the bar.

The crowd parted to let them through, and Dotty, who followed behind Keya and Keely, heard people whispering. It was probably an exciting day for those not directly involved in Roger Dewhirst's death.

They found the tall constable standing beside the reception desk and Keya asked, "Do you know where Inspector Evans is?"

"In the manager's office conducting an interview."

"Is Sergeant Unwin still with him?"

"As far as I know," replied the young constable.

"Can you get him for me?"

When the constable frowned, Keya added, "Tell him Sergeant Varma has another suspect for him to interview."

Recognition appeared to dawn on the constable's face and he turned away quickly and knocked on a door behind the reception desk.

After a whispered conversation with one of the occupants, he returned with Sergeant Unwin.

"This is Roger Dewhirst's girlfriend, Keely Clarke," introduced Keya.

"Oh good. That saves me having to look for her. The inspector has nearly finished with Mrs Wright, and she told us all about her husband's girlfriend."

Dotty thought Natalie only discovered her husband was cheating on her today, but had she known about Keely for a while?

"Thief," cried a man.

The three police officers and Dotty turned quickly in the direction of the shout. An elderly man with shaggy grey hair and beard appeared from the bar area and again yelled, "Thief!"

"Where?" questioned Keya. "I don't see anyone running away or acting suspiciously. At least, no more than they were a minute ago."

Keely sagged down in an armchair beside the reception desk.

Sergeant Unwin stepped towards the shouting man and, in an authoritative voice, instructed, "Sir, please stop shouting. I'm a police officer. Come and discuss your allegations with myself and my colleague."

The shaggy-grey-haired man rushed towards the reception desk and exclaimed, "At last. All the other policemen and women said they were following orders and couldn't help."

Out of the corner of her eye, Dotty noticed the door behind the reception desk open and Inspector Evans called, "Sergeant. Constable."

Sergeant Unwin glanced behind him at the constable who, obeying the inspector's orders, had reached the partially open door. The sergeant turned back to the grey-haired man and said, "Please speak to my colleague."

As Sergeant Unwin entered the room behind the reception desk, Keely stood up, swayed, and staggered towards the revolving entrance door.

"No, you don't," blurted Keya as she sprang after Keely.

Dotty turned to the shaggy-grey-haired man and said, "Mr?"

"Dickinson. Ernie Dickinson."

"And you've seen a thief?"

"Seen him? No. If I had, I wouldn't be bothering you lot. I'm quite capable of dealing with scoundrels on my own. No, someone has stolen from my stall and I've no idea who it is. You'll have to search everyone, and make sure nobody leaves until my property is returned."

Ernie Dickinson must have lost something extremely valuable to be making such a scene.

In a soothing tone, Dotty explained, "As you probably know, another stallholder died today and the police are tied up with that investigation."

Keya returned, dragging an unwilling Keely who she gently but firmly pushed back into the armchair. "Stay there until the inspector asks for you."

"So you're not the police?" A redness entered Ernie's cheeks.

Dotty also felt a flush rise in her own face as she replied, "I'm a consultant."

"And I'm Sergeant Varma," added Keya, still keeping one eye on Keely.

"Sergeant Varma," called Sergeant Unwin. "Please bring Miss .... for her interview with the inspector."

The young constable appeared from the room behind the reception desk, leading Natalie, whose head was bowed.

Before they reached the revolving doors, Natalie's friends stepped forward, and the one with the red shoes asked, "Have you finished?"

Natalie nodded her head.

"I've been instructed to drive her home," stated the constable proudly.

"No need for that. I can drive." The friend with the navy chiffon dress linked her arm through Natalie's and pulled her towards the hotel entrance.

The young constable remained rooted to the spot as he watched them leave.

"So Mr ...?" said Keya, slightly breathlessly, as she rejoined Dotty and Ernie.

"Ernie Dickinson. I've been robbed."

CHAPTER THIRTEEN

Dotty and Keya followed Ernie Dickinson through the still packed bar area of Charbury Castle Hotel.

A theft at an antique fair fell within the remit of the Rural, Heritage and Wildlife Unit which Keya worked for.

Dotty glanced at the bar's occupants and caught the eye of a young woman with dark, spiky hair who held a spiral-bound notepad in one hand. Her mobile phone was in the other hand and she held it up towards the man talking beside her. Was she recording him? Dotty wondered.

"I think the press are here," she confided to Keya as they stepped outside. Dotty was jolted by a gust of biting wind, but at least it cleared her slightly stuffy head.

"I think it's going to rain again," remarked Keya as they both pulled their jackets tighter around them.

"Your lot sealed off the first marquee, but there's a makeshift entrance into the second one," Ernie informed them, and they followed him into the middle marquee.

It was much busier than the last time Keya and Dotty had been in, looking around the stalls.

At the top end, people kept stopping to stare through the closed glass-panelled door into the tent beyond, where Roger Dewhirst's body had been found.

"Excuse me," called Ernie, as he pushed his way through a group of chatting women to a stall Dotty recognised from her visit to the fair at Bath Showground.

It displayed copper and brass jugs, bowls and plates, and David had stopped to examine some of them.

"There!" exclaimed Ernie, pointing to the orange tablecloth.

Keya raised her eyebrows and asked, "What am I looking at?"

"The empty space where my jug and dish were displayed."

"Are you saying that the items stolen from your stall were displayed here?" inquired Dotty.

The space Ernie pointed to was towards the middle of his stall, so the thief must have leaned over to pick them up. It would have been much easier to just grab one or two objects from the front and make a quick getaway.

"Yes, a beautiful copper jug and an engraved Islamic brass plate."

"Valuable then?" asserted Keya, as she removed her notepad from her patchwork sling bag.

"The plate was worth £500 and the jug I was selling for £350, although it might have been worth more," mused Ernie.

"Why do you say that?" Keya looked up from writing in her notepad.

"A couple of Arab looking gentleman took a fancy to it at another fair."

"But they didn't buy it?"

The stallholder shook his head, and Keya made another note.

"I'm not sure there's much more I can do. I'll ask one of the constables to enter the details on our system and provide you with a crime reference number for insurance purposes." Keya snapped closed her notebook.

"Is that it?" Ernie's face took on a pinched expression.

"Sergeant Varma," called a voice from the marquee's temporary entrance.

"Excuse me," said Keya, moving away.

Dotty did not follow her friend but instead said to Ernie, "I'm afraid the police are rather preoccupied with Roger Dewhirst's death."

Ernie gulped. "Of course. Do they know what happened to him?"

Dotty hesitated. She didn't want to divulge any details she shouldn't, but if she was right, and the press were already asking question, everyone would soon know.

Dotty lowered her voice and whispered, "He was stabbed."

"No!" Ernie ran a hand through his shaggy grey hair. "Mind you, he's ruffled a few feathers recently."

"What do you mean?" asked Dotty.

"People always presume stallholders like myself are dodgy, and Roger was one of those that fuelled that reputation. He wasn't straight with the public. Nor with others in the business. If I was the police, I'd be looking for someone in the antiques trade with a grievance against him. There's only so much people in this game will take."

"Did you know him well?" pressed Dotty.

"Not any more than the other stallholders I see each weekend. Enough to stop and have a beer with, but I don't know anything about him personally, apart from his partner, Keely."

"Did you know he was married?"

"To Keely?" Ernie raised his eyebrows.

"No, someone else."

"Now that does make sense."

There was a short silence, so Dotty returned to the original discussion and asked, "What were the pieces like that were taken? I work at Akemans and I'm learning about antiques."

Ernie slipped his hands into his trouser pockets as he regarded Dotty with what she thought was an uneasy expression.

Ignoring it, she continued, "I help in the antiques centre and organise the monthly auctions."

Ernie looked into the distance as he recounted, "The plate was brass, about 30 cm in diameter, with scalloped edging and geometric, floral, and Arabic calligraphy designs. It was clearly Islamic, early twentieth century and probably from Egypt."

He paused before continuing. "And the jug was delicately engraved copper-gilt with a crescent-shaped top and a long, flattened spout. I thought it was a twentieth century reproduction of an ancient Persian piece, but I'm not so sure now. What if it was the original? It would be very valuable."

Dotty doubted it was. If the jug had been an ancient priceless artefact, then surely someone would have snapped it up, buying it either for themselves, knowing they had claimed a fantastic bargain, or selling it on at a huge profit.

"When did you realise they were missing?" asked Dotty.

"After someone, I think it was Ethel, or was it Edith, shouted out that Roger was dead."

"So you know Ethel and Edith?"

"Oh yes, and the game they play. And I'll admit, I've used them when I've seen a client wavering. If the piece is worth it, I'm happy to give them a cut. They were around this morning, before Roger's body was discovered, and even looked at some objects on my stall, but Edith … or is it Ethel …? the one with the straight hair seemed distracted."

"What happened when one of them shouted about Roger?"

"I, and most of the other people in here, rushed to the opening between the two marquees. We had a look, couldn't see much, and had a bit of a chat. It was only after I'd returned to my stall and customers started looking around again that I realised there was a gap, and that the plate and jug had been stolen."

"Did you ask the other stallholders if they'd seen anything?"

"I did, but like me, they'd been preoccupied with the announcement of Roger's death. And nobody noticed anyone hanging around my stall."

Dotty sighed and glanced towards the temporary entrance. "I'm sorry for your loss, and I'll keep a lookout at Akemans in case either item appears."

Keya stood in the temporary entrance and called, "Dotty."

CHAPTER FOURTEEN

After the excitement of the antique fair, Dotty slept in on Sunday morning. She made herself a cup of tea in the small kitchen of her cottage at Meadowbank Farm and carried it back upstairs to her bedroom.

Earl Grey joined her as she climbed into bed, and he snuggled down on the duvet beside her.

She picked up the three books on gold and silver hallmarks, collecting pottery and porcelain, and Babylonian antiquities, which she'd bought the previous day, and began flicking through them.

Weak sunlight filtered through her daisy-patterned curtains and although the rain had woken her during the night, the wind no longer drove it against her windowpanes. Earl Grey stretched his legs out.

"Have you been fed?" she asked as she tickled him under his chin. He leaned his head back and purred.

Eventually, Dotty dragged herself to the shower and then dressed in a pair of jeans with a blue and white striped long sleeve t-shirt and a navy zip-fronted fleece.

Earl Grey followed her down the stairs and through the connecting door into the main farmhouse. She entered the empty kitchen and wondered at the unusual Sunday morning silence.

Then she remembered that Norman had been studying an

Ordnance Survey map the previous evening, and he'd said that if the weather was fine, he was taking himself walking. It was all part of discovering himself.

Dotty wandered over to the pine kitchen table where Aunt Beanie had written a note in large green felt-tip letters. "Gone to Church. Back between 12 and 1. Chicken in fridge. Sunday lunch at 2 pm?"

Dotty smiled. It had become a tradition that when she, Aunt Beanie and Norman were all at home, they'd sit down to a roast Sunday dinner. And sometimes they asked Keya. Dotty wondered if she was free today.

"Hiya," said Keya, answering her phone.

"What are you doing today?"

"Looking for an excuse not to clean my house. I'm standing on my worktop, and I can't believe how dirty the tops of my kitchen units are."

"Why are you cleaning them?" Dotty felt guilty, as she'd never cleaned the top of her kitchen units. Mind you, she usually cooked in the farmhouse kitchen.

"It's this course I'm doing. It makes me feel that to be a proper cook, my own kitchen has to be pristine."

"Well, when you've finished, why don't you come over for lunch? We're aiming to eat at two as long as Norman is back from his hike. We're having chicken. Do you have anything you could bring, or do I need to go shopping?"

"I've some pinto bean chilli left over from Thursday night. I was going to eat that today, but it'll be so much better with a Yorkshire pudding and some roast potatoes."

"I'll be in the rest of the morning if you get bored with cleaning and want to come over," suggested Dotty.

She finished the call and walked across to the blue Aga range cooker, lifted the cover from a hot plate and pulled the chrome kettle across to it. She'd start with a cup of tea.

Dotty was peeling potatoes when she thought she heard the doorbell ring. Nobody ever used it. Visitors knocked on the front door and strode into the house, or just strode in and knocked on the kitchen door.

The bell rang again.

Dotty rinsed her hands and dried them on a grey towel hanging from the chrome rail which ran in front of the Aga.

As the ringing became more insistent, she quickened her pace along the terracotta tiled corridor to the entrance door and flung it open. Had something happened to Norman?

"Yes?" she asked breathlessly.

"Dorothy Sayers?" enquired a young woman with spiky black hair. Was she the same girl - she only looked eighteen or nineteen - Dotty had seen in the bar at Charbury Castle Hotel? The one she'd thought was a reporter?

"Yes," Dotty replied, more hesitantly now.

"Ozzie Winters, from the Cirencester Times." The girl thrust forward her hand, which held a white business card.

Gingerly, Dotty took the card and asked, "How can I help you?"

"You were there yesterday? At the antique fair?"

Dotty didn't reply.

"And I saw you talking to the police, which either makes you a suspect, or someone they trust. A consultant, for instance?"

"If I was, I wouldn't be allowed to speak to journalists," Dotty replied primly. "I suggest you contact Gloucestershire Police's media department."

Ozzie inclined her head. "You know I'll get nothing out of them."

Dotty shuffled her feet. "I'm sorry, I don't know anything about the man who died and I can't help you. I must go as I'm making lunch. Goodbye."

Dotty hastily closed the door as Ozzie called, "You can call or message me anytime. I only want the same thing as you. Justice for the victim and his family."

Dotty wasn't sure what justice Roger's wife Natalie would want beside finding the killer. And what if she had killed him? Perhaps that was her justice for him cheating on her.

Dotty returned to peeling potatoes.

When she finished, she checked her watch. It was quarter past twelve. She'd better prepare the chicken. It needed about an hour and a quarter in the oven, although timings weren't precise with an Aga.

It had taken her some time to get used to an oven which she

couldn't just set at a temperature and know it would remain true and constant.

Aunt Beanie had shown her how to have a better feeling for food and cooking, and to move dishes between the hotter top section of the top oven and the not-so-hot lower section.

And she found the bottom warming oven very useful, especially when cooking lots of dishes, as she would be doing today for the Sunday roast.

Keya arrived just after half-past twelve, as Dotty was sliding the metal roasting dish containing a large chicken into the bottom section of the top oven.

She'd found half a lemon in the fridge and cut several sprigs of thyme from a pot on the conservatory window, and stuffed them inside the bird.

She'd also chopped some celery, onion and carrots and placed them beneath the chicken with a generous portion of white wine to flavour it while cooking, and keep it moist.

"Hiya," greeted Keya. "Where is everyone?"

Earl Grey rubbed against her legs.

"Does he do that on purpose?" she asked as Dotty picked up Earl Grey.

"You know Keya's allergic to you, don't you?" Dotty pretended to scold Earl Grey. "Why don't you go and find Agatha?"

She carried him along the corridor to the front door and placed him on the brown, fraying doormat. His fur swelled in volume and he looked up at Dotty with what she thought was a put-out expression.

"Go on. Off you go and find Agatha."

Earl Grey stalked across the broken tarmac yard, his tail erect.

"Thanks," acknowledged Keya when she returned. "I've taken an antihistamine tablet, but it doesn't always work, especially as Earl Grey's so hairy."

Dotty placed the pan of potatoes on the hottest plate on the Aga. Next, she began chopping a cauliflower. As she did, she remarked, "I've just had a visit from a young journalist for the Cirencester Times."

"A girl called Ozzie something?"

"That's right. I presume she wanted to know about Roger

Dewhirst's death, but I told her I couldn't help, and she'd need to contact the police's media department."

"I bet she was chuffed with that suggestion. They hardly tell me anything, and I'm a police officer."

Dotty picked up the card the reporter had given her and asked, "Do you know her then, Ozzie Winters?"

"I met her recently when she tried to question me about the inhabitants of Lemington. I don't know what's got into them, but they keep picking fights with each other."

Dotty tipped the cauliflower florets into a pan and started chopping carrots into regular-shaped orange batons.

Keya continued, "One of the allotment holders claims another has deliberately poisoned his vegetables, a woman accused another of running her off the road in her new 4x4, and fists were thrown at a parish council meeting when one member refused to endorse another's plans to build an extension over his garage."

Dotty smiled. "Sounds like a typical Cotswold village to me." She added boiling water to the pan of cauliflower and placed it on the hot plate, beside the potatoes.

Using her sharp chopping knife, she stabbed a potato to feel if it was ready. Nearly. There was some give, but she didn't want them falling apart in the oven.

"I know what you mean," agreed Keya, "but villagers don't like their squabbles being made public. They soon banded together when that reporter started asking questions. I was running a road safety course at the local school, and you should have heard the Mums. Normally they argue about which child is best at maths, or running, or they're criticising another child's birthday cake, but when Ozzie turned up, they were all friends and life in the village was idyllic. It was hilarious."

On the cooler of the two hotplates, Dotty melted butter in a smaller pan. She added two spoons of flour and mixed it with the butter to form a thick yellowish paste.

As she did, the kitchen door opened and Aunt Beanie strode in, flinging the Sunday papers on the pine table.

CHAPTER FIFTEEN

Pulling the chair out at the head of the kitchen table, Aunt Beanie sat down and complained, "I thought church was supposed to bring a sense of calm and peace. I feel exhausted, but it might be listening to old Mrs Jenkins grumbling about her arthritis. Apparently, it's particularly bad in this cold, wet weather."

Dotty drained the potatoes, shook the colander to fluff them up, and sprinkled flour over them to absorb some of the moisture.

She'd leave them to steam for a short time while the tray she'd put in the oven, containing a layer of rapeseed oil, heated up.

"Tea?" she asked.

"No thanks. I had at least three cups after church," replied Aunt Beanie.

"Yes, please," replied Keya as she sat down at the table next to Aunt Beanie, facing the Aga. "Cleaning kitchen cupboards is thirsty work."

Dotty pulled the kettle onto the hottest hot plate, next to the boiling cauliflower, and continued adding milk to her thick, creamy sauce.

As she sprinkled powdered nutmeg into the sauce, Aunt Beanie asked, "Any sign of Norman?"

"Not yet," replied Dotty. "How long did he say he'd be?"

"He didn't. I hope he's all right."

Dotty drained the cauliflower, catching the liquid in a bowl, as she'd use it to make gravy later.

Keya remarked, "He's worked outdoors all his life. Surely he's used to walking along tracks?"

Aunt Beanie sighed. "I suppose he should be, but he's so obsessed with 'finding himself' I can just imagine him wandering along, deep in thought, and falling into a quarry or off the Cotswold escarpment."

Dotty pulled the tray of hot rapeseed oil out of the top oven of the Aga. "I'm sure he'll be fine. But ready for lunch."

She tipped the boiled potatoes into the fat, which hissed. Gently she turned each one in turn, using a knife and fork, until they were all covered in oil and placed the tray back in the top oven.

Then she pulled out the chicken.

As Dotty basted it with its own juices mixed with wine and cooking oil, Aunt Beanie picked up a newspaper and flicked through the pages. She announced, "Here we are. Antique dealer stabbed to death with a fork."

"We were trying to keep the details out of the press," groaned Keya.

"Police are baffled ..." read Aunt Beanie.

Dotty looked up and saw Keya wince.

"... by the death of local antique dealer, Roger Dewhirst." Aunt Beanie placed the paper back on the table. "Antique dealer! I've seen Roger around and he's no more than a bric-a-brac salesman. No idea about genuine antiques. Still, he seemed to make a fair living from his trade."

Keya swivelled the open newspaper round to face her, and reported, "His wife was the real money earner. She paid the rent and bills on their four-bedroom house on one of the modern estates on the edge of Cirencester. She runs her own hairdressing salon in the town, 'A Cut Above' on Silver Street. It's quite upmarket."

"I know the place," confirmed Aunt Beanie. "It's been there for years. Used to be called Maureen's."

"I don't know about that," Keya replied.

Dotty looked round the kitchen worktop. The chicken and roast potatoes were in the oven, together with a sage and onion stuffing which she'd prepared from a packet, but which she was keeping separate from the chicken so Keya could also enjoy it.

She'd mixed the cauliflower with the white sauce, tipped it into an oval Pyrex dish and scattered cheese over the top. The batter, which was the consistency of single cream, was resting on the worktop and she just needed to add oil to a cupcake baking tray.

She'd heat it up before pouring a tablespoon of mixture into each hole and praying they would fluff up to create golden Yorkshire puddings.

That left the gravy to mix and the carrots to cook.

The door opened, and a mud splattered Norman staggered in.

Aunt Beanie jumped up and cried, "What happened to you?"

"I slipped climbing down from a stile and landed in a puddle."

"Well, don't stand here dripping onto the floor. Go grab yourself a shower and then we'll be ready to eat."

Norman sniffed the air and his eyes gleamed. "Roast chicken," he mumbled appreciatively before leaving the kitchen.

By the time Norman reappeared in the kitchen, Keya had set the table and Dotty was removing dishes from the oven.

Aunt Beanie was trying her best to carve the chicken, but instead of neat slices, she was cutting off lumps of white meat. "Can you take over?" she asked Norman.

He chuckled and replied, "You're doing a grand job. Besides, I prefer a leg." He opened the fridge and removed a bottle of Wiltshire Gold beer. It hissed when he removed the top with a bottle opener, and he sighed in satisfaction as he poured the frothing golden liquid into a pint glass.

Keya removed her pinto bean chilli from the bottom oven where it had been warming through and emptied it onto a plate.

"Help yourself," instructed Dotty, pointing to the roasting dishes of potatoes, sage and onion stuffing, and perfectly risen Yorkshire puddings. She placed them, and the dishes of cauliflower and carrots, on glass heat-proof mats on the worktop.

"Yummy," exclaimed Keya as she piled up her plate.

"Don't be greedy," chided Aunt Beanie as Norman was about to place a sixth roast potato on his plate. "I know you've had an energetic morning, but there's still Dotty and me to come."

Norman's jaw clenched, but he returned the potato to the roasting dish.

When they were all seated at the dining table, Aunt Beanie looked around and said, "I'd like to say grace."

They all bowed their heads.

"Dear Lord. Thank you for our health and wellbeing, and for blessing our table with this delicious meal. Keep Cliff safe and happy. Amen."

"Amen," the others muttered and tucked into their food.

Keya finished chewing and asked, "Where were you walking, Norman?"

"I've found a route called the Drover's Trail, which begins, or probably ended in medieval times, in Cirencester. I guess shepherds used to walk their sheep to market."

"Was it interesting?" asked Dotty.

"Pleasant, I'd say, with fabulous views, but it was annoying today as I had to walk so far, and then turn round and retrace my steps. I wonder if one of you could pick me up next week and drive me back to the Land Rover? That way I can walk more of the trail."

"I can do that," volunteered Dotty. "Will you walk the rest of the route next week?"

"No," laughed Norman as he picked up his glass. "I think all in all, it'll take about five weeks. It actually starts, or ends, in Evesham."

"I don't think that part of the walk will be particularly interesting," claimed Aunt Beanie.

"You never know what you'll find. Let's see. And I appreciate your offer, Dotty. Thank you."

As Norman ate his next mouthful, he pulled the newspaper, still open at the story about Roger Dewhirst, closer and began reading. When he'd finished chewing, he observed, "So our deceased had been in trouble with the law."

"Had he?" spluttered Keya. "I didn't know that."

"It says here," Norman continued, "that he was arrested six years ago at a car boot sale for selling counterfeit branded clothing. He claimed the items were second-hand, and he had no idea they were fakes, and the police released him with a caution."

Keya was chewing slowly. "How did the paper find out about that?" she wondered out loud.

Norman glanced at the article. "The reporter's called Ozzie Winters."

Dotty looked up. "She came here today."

"Really?" Aunt Beanie blurted, her fork hovering halfway to her mouth.

"Yes. She said she writes for the Cirencester Times."

"So a piece in a National Sunday paper will be a coup for her. What did she want?" Aunt Beanie's fork reached her mouth, and she started chewing.

"Inside information on Roger Dewhirst's death. I saw her in the bar at Charbury Castle Hotel, and she must have seen me with the police. She thought I'd have the inside track."

"Which you usually do," conceded Keya.

"Anyway, I told her I couldn't help."

Aunt Beanie moved the cut end of a roast potato around her plate to soak up some gravy. "You'll have to watch out now you're on a reporter's radar. They have a habit of catching you unaware. Be careful."

There was silence around the table.

Norman placed his knife and fork together on his plate and sighed with satisfaction.

"That was wonderful, Dotty. Just what I needed. But you're not going to spend the rest of your life cooking for Aunt Beanie and I, are you? What do you want to do with your life?"

"Leave the girl alone," remonstrated Aunt Beanie.

"No, it's OK," replied Dotty. "I do need to consider what I want to do. So far, I've just gone along with what other people wanted. At least what the men in my life have wanted." She lowered her head and stared at the table.

Keya touched her arm. "Nothing that's happened has been your fault."

"But I have been a passive participant. Norman's right. I need to work out what I want, and how to get it."

Aunt Beanie sat up and waved her hand in a dismissive gesture. "All this talk about finding something in the future. What about the here and now? What could be better than sitting round a table on a Sunday afternoon, sharing a fabulous meal with friends? Let's raise a glass to our cook."

Dotty looked up and smiled warmly at Aunt Beanie, Keya, and Norman as they lifted their glasses and toasted, "To Dotty."

CHAPTER SIXTEEN

When Dotty arrived at Akemans on Monday morning, Marion Rook, David's wife, was already seated at the reception desk. As usual, she looked immaculate with sleek bobbed grey hair, under which her purple-red ruby earrings flashed when they caught the light.

She stood up and Dotty admired her tailored herringbone tweed trousers, which matched her short purple cardigan, worn over a cream blouse.

"Morning Dotty. I'll fetch David," said Marion. "He's in the main auction room discussing this month's sale with George."

Dotty remained standing, fidgeting with her hands and uncertain what to do now that Marion had taken over her desk.

"Good morning, Dorothy," greeted David as he entered the reception, alone.

"Gainfords are having a five-day sale of a private collection this week. Over a thousand decorative and fine art pieces. I thought we could take a trip to London tomorrow for the Indian and Ottoman art, jewellery, and textiles section of the sale. And spend today researching the pieces and the eras they are from."

Dotty remained rooted to the spot. The sale sounded fascinating, but to return to Gainfords? She wasn't sure about that.

"David, have some consideration for the girl," admonished Marion, returning to the reception area. "Gainfords doesn't hold the fondest memories for Dotty, does it, my dear?"

Dotty slowly shook her head.

"Tea?" enquired Marion. "Or would you like to sample our coffee?" Marion and David preferred a rich coffee with a cardamom flavour. It smelt wonderful but Dotty didn't fancy it at the moment.

"A cup of tea would be great," she replied.

"You two sit down on the sofa and I'll bring your drinks over. Go gentle with Dotty, David, and remember, she doesn't have an encyclopaedic memory of Ottoman history," reminded Marion.

"I'm not even sure who the Ottomans are," Dotty admitted.

"Ah well," and David spent half an hour explaining the history and geography of the Ottoman Empire, helped by information he found on Akemans' company tablet.

But Dotty was captivated when he started showing her incredible Ottoman treasures, from ornate gold jewellery, to jewel encrusted armour, to fine silk fabrics.

"What's being sold tomorrow?" she asked.

David tapped the tablet and brought up the entries for the next day's auction. Each one had a photograph, a brief description and an estimated value, which were all at least four figures, and some were considerably higher.

There were lots of paintings and woven or painted silk wall hangings, several ornate boxes and even an ancient chess set from Jaipur, India, with miniature archers and figures riding elephants.

"That's beautiful," said Dotty, admiring the chess set. "But who would want to play with it? The pieces look so delicate."

"I doubt anyone has recently, but back in the palace, I'm sure the Raja of Jaipur once did."

As Dotty examined a pair of gold embroidered silk boots, David's phone rang.

He answered it and listened. "Yes, Chief Inspector. I'll come straight away."

David finished the call and explained, "Chief Inspector Ringrose has asked to see me about an object stolen at Saturday's antique fair."

"The brass plate or copper jug?" asked Dotty.

"I'm not sure, but how do you know about them?" David looked at her sharply.

"I was at the fair on Saturday. I ..." she was about to add that she saw David leaving but for some reason didn't. "I spoke to the stallholder. It was the same jug you picked up at the fair at Bath Showground."

"Was it?" David replied airily. "I can't remember. I see so many objects at those fairs. But as you know so much, you had better come with me."

David drove Dotty to Cirencester in his vintage silver Mercedes and they parked in a visitors' space outside the modern Cotswold-stone clad police station.

As Dotty climbed out of the car, she remembered the first time she'd been inside the station. It was at Norman's request, to collect and look after Earl Grey, who had originally belonged to the late Duke of Ditchford, when the police took Norman in for questioning.

Although Norman had been released without charge, Earl Grey had stayed with Dotty.

They entered the front reception, which smelt faintly of vomit and strongly of disinfectant. It must have been a busy weekend with the students back at the agricultural college.

Dotty glanced at those waiting. They were mostly respectable looking middle-aged or elderly people and she realised she recognised some of them as stallholders from Saturday's antique fair.

David spoke to the grey-haired officer standing behind the Perspex screen. "David Rook and Dorothy Sayers to see Chief Inspector Ringrose."

Dotty spotted the brown-suited Inspector Evans over the officer's shoulder and involuntarily took a step back.

She could tell he was angry - perhaps by his wide stance and the way his chin jutted out - and he was berating the young uniformed constable who'd been keeping guard while Natalie Wright was interviewed at the antique fair.

"I don't care. She found out before us!" she heard the inspector shout.

The elderly officer manning the reception turned and called, "PC Jenkins. Please can you escort our guests to Chief Inspector Ringrose?"

Dotty wondered if it was his way of saving the young officer from the irate inspector.

He turned back to David and pushed two blue lanyards with 'visitor' written in large letters on the attached white badges and instructed, "Please wear these whilst in the building."

A buzzing noise signalled the door into the main building was unlocked and David pushed it open.

Dotty followed but was relieved to find Inspector Evans had disappeared, presumably back to his office.

PC Jenkins led them up a flight of concrete stairs, the central section covered with a cheap blue nylon carpet, to the first floor.

"I take it the inspector found out about the article in Sunday's newspaper?" Dotty asked PC Jenkins.

"Yes, ma'am." PC Jenkins remained stiff-lipped.

"And he blamed you for it? I saw the reporter, Ozzie Winters, speaking to the occupants of the hotel bar on Sunday afternoon."

"So that's how she found out," blurted the young officer.

"Once a few of the stallholders had their tongues loosened by a couple of drinks, they'd be more than happy to tell a young, attractive journalist all they knew."

PC Jenkins blushed.

Did he have a thing for Ozzie Winters?

"It certainly wasn't your fault," she continued. "Is that why you're interviewing the stallholders again?"

The young constable stopped and turned to Dotty. "How did you know?"

"I recognised a few of them waiting in reception."

PC Jenkins lowered his voice and revealed, "The inspector's starting with those in the marquee where the body was found. He's interviewing them to discover if they saw anything connected to Mr Dewhirst's death, and what they knew about the deceased, his wife, girlfriend, and anyone else connected to him. It's going to take all day."

PC Jenkins led them along a corridor and through a door towards the rear of the building. The first person they met was Aunt Beanie.

"I wondered if you'd accompany David," she remarked.

"You didn't say you were coming in today." Dotty felt put out, although she knew she shouldn't.

"Sorry, I forgot to tell you that I was asked to help out as Keya, Sergeant Varma, is away on her baking course. And there's growing interest in the items stolen at the antique fair, which is why we wanted David's expert opinion. Come through to the chief inspector's office."

Dotty turned to PC Jenkins and said, "Thank you, and good luck with the interviews."

The young PC gave her a grimace of a smile in response.

There were only a handful of desks in the open-plan space which reached to the back of the building, but a mountain of grey boxes were piled on top of each other at the far end.

Aunt Beanie followed Dotty's gaze and confided, "Old cases. Many of them unsolved, which the chief inspector and I want to get to the bottom of. But for now ..." she opened the door to the chief inspector's office, which occupied a corner position in the room.

Chief Inspector Ringrose sat back as they entered and folded his arms. He wore a blue and white checked shirt with a green tie which had some sort of motif embroidered on it.

"Welcome. Good of you to come, David. And I see you've brought Dorothy with you. Please take a seat."

Dotty had expected a warmer welcome from Chief Inspector Ringrose. Was it her imagination, or did he seem irritated by her presence? She shook her head. She must be imagining it, as she'd always had an amicable relationship with the chief inspector.

Dotty, Aunt Beanie and David sat down on blue fabric chairs with pale wooden arms.

The chief inspector strolled round to the front of his desk and handed out colour photographs of the copper jug and brass plate.

He returned to his desk and perched on it, facing his audience. "Of course, Dorothy, you were at the crime scene on Saturday. Did you speak to the stallholder, Ernie Dickinson, about the items which were stolen? He's been kicking up quite a fuss."

"He was like that on Saturday," confirmed Dotty. "And the jug, which David and I saw the previous week ..." She felt David stiffen beside her. "... was attractive, but if, as Ernie thought, it was a twentieth century reproduction, not particularly valuable."

"That's the thing," the chief inspector disclosed. "He now thinks it was a much earlier piece, and worth far more."

"Probably after the insurance money," dismissed David.

"You'd seen the jug before. What were your thoughts about it, David?" asked the chief inspector.

"Dorothy has a better memory than me. I don't remember the jug, so I doubt it was anything special. I'd be very surprised if it was an original."

"But if it was?" pressed the chief inspector.

David swallowed and examined the photograph of the jug. "Then I'd say it was from the time of the Zand Dynasty, which ruled modern day Iran and much of Iraq between 1751 and 1779."

"Old then," remarked Aunt Beanie, "But not an ancient Persian or Babylonian artefact."

"No," agreed David.

"And its value, if it were from that era?" asked the chief inspector.

"£25,000 to £30,000, at a guess. I'm not sure I've seen anything similar on the market for a while, and I've no idea what condition it was in."

David looked up at the chief inspector, who crossed his arms. "So a jug was stolen, which was either a twentieth century reproduction, worth a few hundred pounds, or an eighteenth century original worth at least twenty-five thousand. What are we going to file on the police report?"

There was silence in the room.

Dotty wet her lips and said, "Ernie was never going to get a huge amount for the jug, as he was only selling it for the smaller sum. It's only because it's been stolen that he's questioning its value. And our discussion has been speculation. His description and original value should be given to the insurers."

"Well put," agreed David. "An attractive jug, but nothing special about it."

Dotty glanced at him and thought she saw a sheen of sweat on his forehead.

Did he really believe the jug was only a reproduction?

Dotty was asked to wait outside the chief inspector's office while he, David, and Aunt Beanie discussed other matters.

PC Jenkins appeared and said, "I've been asked to escort you downstairs."

Dotty glanced behind her and replied, "We'll be ready in a few minutes when David has finished his meeting. How are the interviews going?"

The constable's round boyish face relaxed, and he grinned. "The inspector's in a much better mood and has just left to arrest Natalie Wright, the wife."

"What? Why?"

"One of the ladies we interviewed said she saw the deceased arguing with a blonde woman. The witness did wear thick, round glasses, but she was adamant the woman wasn't Keely, the girlfriend, who she knew well, but an older, well-dressed woman, who wore proper trousers rather than jeans, as is the fashion now she said."

"But is that a reason to arrest Natalie?"

"If she was there, arguing with her husband, then her story that she drove away and didn't return until later falls apart."

Dotty remembered she and Keya also saw Roger arguing with a woman when they re-entered the first marquee. They'd bought the books, looked at a few more stalls, and gone for lunch, so the argument probably took place thirty to forty minutes before Roger's body was found.

The young police constable was right. If Natalie had been arguing with her husband, she couldn't have been driving, and her alibi was a lie.

CHAPTER SEVENTEEN

David arrived at Meadowbank Farm on Tuesday morning at seven o'clock.

It was still dark as Dotty walked over to his car and called, "Bye," to Norman as he walked across the yard towards the barn with a torch, presumably to milk Buttercup.

"What? Oh, bye," Norman replied sleepily.

"I'm not sure what time I'll be back, but I'll call when we're leaving London." Dotty climbed into David's car and said a warm, "Morning."

"You're much brighter than I expected. Marion instructed me to treat you gently this morning, as we're returning to Gainfords."

"I had a long chat with Aunt Beanie last night and she's right, Gainfords had nothing to do with any of this, and how well did I really know Gilmore, anyway? A couple of dinners and a Christmas kiss under the mistletoe. It's my pride and my confidence which took the real battering. So no more men for a while, and plenty of time to concentrate on work and learning the antique trade."

"Glad to hear it," proclaimed David as he drove out of the farmyard.

The journey along the M4 motorway passed quickly but uneventfully, apart from queues for the junctions outside Reading.

Marion had been right. David had an encyclopaedic knowledge

and not just about the Ottoman Empire, but antiques in general, and particularly those from the Middle East and Asia. Dotty enjoyed talking to him.

He drove into the centre of London and parked outside an impressive three-storey terraced house with a white stone frontage at ground floor level, and exposed brick walls above.

"This property belongs to a friend of mine," explained David. "He let's me park here when I visit London."

It was certainly convenient. They walked down the street, turned a corner, and waited for a gap in the traffic before crossing the road. Two minutes later they arrived at Gainfords, in St James's.

The neo-classical building was grand and elegant, with a columned entrance. The black metal planters resting on ledges, below the long casement windows, contained dwarf conifers rather than the colourful flowers Dotty had seen during the summer months.

A red-liveried doorman ushered them inside an impressive entrance hall with a high, moulded ceiling and an oak staircase leading to the first floor, with elegantly carved wooden balusters.

David placed his hand on Dotty's back and guided her towards the staircase. "Today's sale items will be on display next to the auction room on the first floor."

Although Gainfords had only just opened, a crowd of people were already looking around the sale items which were expertly displayed in glass cases or hung on the walls.

Most people were viewing the jewellery and bright enamelled boxes, so, while David stopped to talk to a member of Gainfords' staff, Dotty wandered into a room with silk wall hangings, embroidered cushions, and other textiles.

Her attention was drawn to three robes. She opened her catalogue and remembered David telling her they were chapan robes, which were like coats and worn over clothes during the cold winter months.

The three in front of her were believed to originate from Iran, Iraq, or Afghanistan.

The first was red silk, brocaded with gold and silver thread, and lined with red Russian cotton. Although it was beautiful, it was quite modern, from the late nineteenth century, and was only - though well out of Dotty's league - valued at £2,000 to £2,500.

The second chapan robe was from the same era, but it was less valuable and made from silk and cotton in green, mauve and pale blue edged with purple silk. The third one was older, and made from purple velvet woven with yellow, red and white chevrons.

"Which do you like best?" asked David as he joined her.

"The red brocade one. It shimmers in the light."

"I agree. Now, come with me. One of the staff has agreed to show us the chess set. It's not on display to the public."

The chess set was even more impressive up close than in the photographs she'd seen, even inside its protective glass display case.

The tallest figurines were only three inches high, and they were magnificent miniature elephants with ornate tented carriages on top, like those used by Indian Maharaja's.

All the figurines were richly enamelled in emerald-green, cobalt-blue, pink and yellow, and were inlaid with diamond chips.

Dotty was still gazing at the chess set when she heard a man call, "Ladies and gentlemen, five minutes."

David led her to the main auction room and found them both seats halfway down the room, beside the central aisle.

The taupe-coloured walls of the auction room gave it a modern feeling and the two chandeliers which hung from the ceiling felt out of place.

A bank of desks formed a row along the left wall, each with a computer screen and several telephones. Behind the auctioneer's rostrum, a large screen hung down with 'Gainfords' displayed on it, and beside it was a large television screen.

A lady wearing a red jacket climbed onto the rostrum and two assistants sat behind her. The image on the screen changed to show a pair of marble, lotus-shaped jardinieres from India.

"Who'll start me at £2,000?" asked the amplified voice of the auctioneer.

Together, David and Dotty watched the first items being auctioned until David started fidgeting in his seat and tapping his fingers against his brochure. He glanced across at a young woman who was manning one of the telephones at the side of the auction room.

She nodded back at David.

"Lot 37, a red silk brocade chapan with metallic silver and gold thread," announced the auctioneer. It was the coat that Dotty liked.

The opening bid was only £500, but the bidding gathered momentum until it stalled at £1,650.

David nodded at the telephone woman and Dotty watched as she spoke into her headpiece, rather than the handset in front of her, before raising her hand.

"£1,700," proclaimed the auctioneer.

Bidding continued with David signalling to the telephone girl before she spoke into her headset. She secured the final bid at £2,300, well within the estimated value.

Beside her, David sighed with relief.

She was about to ask him about the chapan when he jumped to his feet and asked, "Will you be all right on your own? I've some business to attend to."

Dotty spent the rest of the morning on her own. She didn't mind as David's tuition the day before helped her understand more about the articles being sold, their history and their values.

At the coffee break, she left the auction room. She searched for David while she sipped her tea and nibbled on a shortbread biscuit, but she didn't see any sign of him.

At the end of the morning session, she filed out of the room and made her way down to the buffet lunch, which was being provided in one of the ground-floor rooms. She was just biting into a smoked salmon and cream cheese sandwich when David appeared by her side.

"Have you nearly finished?"

It was clear she still had three dainty triangular sandwiches on her plate, a sausage roll, and two cakes.

"Five minutes?" she asked hopefully.

"Very well," he replied distractedly. "I'll meet you in the entrance hall."

Dotty tried not to rush the rest of her lunch, but it didn't taste the same, and she left the sausage roll. She wrapped the cakes in a white paper serviette which she placed in her bag.

Outside, in the entrance hall, she found David talking to Tariq, the young Arab man she'd met at Bath Showground.

He smiled at Dotty as he said to David, "I'll sort that out," and then strode across to the wooden staircase.

David turned to Dotty. He looked relaxed and content. "I have a special treat for you. I've just spoken to the British Museum and they're willing to give us a tour of their Scientific Research Department. We're very lucky, as it's not open to the public."

David hailed a black cab and directed it to the British Museum. Even in January, there was a queue snaking its way towards the museum's public entrance.

David gave his name to a security guard who stood beside a small discrete door, hidden in the shadow of a classical Greek-style stone column, one of many constructed along the entire frontage of the building. The guard checked the paper on his black clipboard before opening the door so they could enter.

David seemed to know his way around as he headed straight for a stone staircase, and they descended into the museum's basement.

"Welcome," said a middle-aged woman whose mousey-brown hair was tied back in a ponytail from which strands were escaping. She pushed a hair behind her ear as she turned and led them into a low-ceilinged room.

There were no windows, but plenty of equipment, although the only piece Dotty recognised was a microscope.

The woman led them to a white laminated table in the centre of the room and said, "These are some of the tiles from the collection you identified at Cotswold Airport." She wore white latex gloves and carefully picked up one of the small tiles. "See this blackened edge?"

Dotty nodded.

"That's from a fire. The tablets were formed from wet clay and the characters imprinted on them with a reed stylus. They would have been left to dry in the sun, which would make them brittle. But these are much stronger. They could have been fired, but from these soot marks, we believe they were in a building which was set alight."

"What does that mean?" asked Dotty.

"That it's very difficult to determine their age. Normally we'd use radiocarbon dating but for that we need organic matter. Anything trapped in these tiles was destroyed during the fire."

"So you don't know how old they are."

The woman smiled. "I didn't say that. We are using other tiles and stones from different periods to date them by comparing the script, both in terms of layout and content."

She moved to the far end of the table and continued, "We're currently comparing them with this fragment of a Babylonian clay tablet, and there are definite similarities."

"Are there more tablets like this displayed in the museum?" asked Dotty.

"Oh, this one isn't on display. It's stored in our vaults."

David grunted in disapproval.

The scientist showed Dotty some of the museum's scientific equipment, including a vibrational spectroscopy, and how they used multispectral imaging techniques to help with the conservation of paintings.

Dotty was relieved when she and David finally stepped outside the museum, and she sucked in a lungful of air. "That was fascinating, but my brain is full."

"Come on," commanded David. His relaxed, content manner of earlier had been replaced by a much darker mood. Dotty ran to catch up as he hailed a black cab.

CHAPTER EIGHTEEN

On Wednesday morning, Dotty wandered down to the farmhouse kitchen.

"There you are Earl Grey." Her furry grey cat didn't even look up from his bowl of cat food.

He was given meat and jelly in the morning and biscuits in the evening, supplemented by leftovers or titbits that she and Aunt Beanie gave him when Norman wasn't looking.

She pulled the chrome kettle onto the hotplate as Norman walked in, wearing a knitted blue hat. "It's blustery out there this morning."

He looked at Dotty, who was wearing her navy fleece over her blue tartan pyjamas. "Aren't you going to be late for work?"

"I'm not sure what to do. Marion is in the office organising next week's auction, as I'm supposed to be shadowing David, but he didn't say anything when he dropped me off yesterday."

"Done something to upset him?"

"Me?" Her throat tightened.

"I'm only joking," grunted Norman. "Watch out, the kettle's boiled. Can you pour me a coffee while I make sure Beanie's getting up? She said she has to pop into the police station this morning."

Dotty made tea for herself and Aunt Beanie, and a white coffee for Norman, and placed them on the kitchen table. Norman reappeared, followed by Aunt Beanie, who slumped down in the chair at the head of the table and rested her head on her arm.

"I'm not used to these working hours," she yawned.

"Aren't you enjoying your job?" asked Dotty.

"Oh yes," Aunt Beanie replied in a brighter tone and reached for her mug of tea as Dotty sat down at the table.

"Bacon sandwiches?" asked Norman.

Aunt Beanie sipped her tea before replying. "Perfect."

"Anything interesting happen at the station yesterday?" asked Dotty.

"Inspector Evans was in a good mood all afternoon. He's arrested Natalie Wright for killing her husband."

"Because a witness said she saw Natalie arguing with her husband when Natalie said she was driving her car?" queried Dotty.

"Oh, you already knew about that." Aunt Beanie narrowed her lips into a thin line, looking put out.

"Not about the arrest," replied Dotty quickly. "That is interesting. PC Jenkins told me about the witness when he escorted David and I on Monday morning."

Aunt Beanie looked appeased as she nodded and sipped her tea.

The smell of frying bacon filled the air and Earl Grey jumped onto Dotty's lap but sat up, staring at the table, rather than curling up and falling asleep. Was he anticipating the arrival of his second breakfast?

Norman placed plates of open sandwiches of bacon on malted brown bread on the pine table. He returned with knives and tomato ketchup, and a packet of mixed lettuce leaves which Dotty liked to add to her sandwich.

"Don't feed that cat any," warned Norman. "He's spoilt. And he's getting fat."

"It's just his fur," defended Dotty. "He develops more of it in the winter to keep him warm."

Norman stopped and stared at Earl Grey, who regarded him calmly with his large yellow eyes.

Norman shook his head and sat down. When he finished chewing a mouthful of sandwich, he said, "If you're at a loose end, can you drive Beanie into Cirencester? Marion wants me at Akemans as soon as possible this morning."

"Sure." Dotty wondered if she could wrangle another visit inside Cirencester police station to find out more about Natalie Wright's arrest.

"I'm only going in for one meeting," Aunt Beanie explained. "Do you have any shopping to do?"

"I'm sure I could find something to occupy me for an hour or so." Dotty wondered what market, if any, was being held in the Corn Hall.

"Excellent, that's all it should take."

Aunt Beanie directed Dotty to park in one of the spaces marked with 'RHW' on a small sign, next to a smart black Land Rover Discovery.

"That's Chief Inspector Ringrose's car and the only other person who parks here is Keya, so you should be fine leaving your car until you pick me up. See you in an hour or so?"

Dotty watched Aunt Beanie enter the police station before turning away, walking down the side of the building past The Bear Inn, and onto Dyer Street.

As she turned towards Market Place, she glanced across at the alley leading to The Woolmarket and the life-size statue of a ram. She shivered. The ram had been the crime scene in another murder.

Her feet led her not to the historic Corn Hall but past the Gothic double-storey stone tower at the entrance to St John Baptist Church, at the end of Market Place.

She continued walking along Castle Street where, apart from Clarks shoe shop, most of the retail units were independently run and she guessed had occupied the same premises for many years. There was a double-fronted jewellers, a small camera and photographic shop, and an optician.

She crossed the road opposite the Black Horse Pub and entered Silver Street. It was much narrower and darker than Castle Street and as the sand-coloured Range Rover coming towards her took up the whole road, she presumed it was a one-way street.

She almost walked past the entrance to Natalie's hair salon but a discreet brown sign, matching the colour of the stone building frontage, positioned between two large casement windows, caught her eye. 'A Cut Above Hair Salon' was written in white letters and there was an image of a pair of scissors.

She retraced her steps to the stone arched entrance and walked inside.

"Can I help you?" asked one of the ladies who'd been with Natalie at the antique fair. Today she wore bright yellow heels rather than red ones.

She finished tidying magazines on a glass coffee table and strode across to a semi-circular reception desk. The room was small and there were no washbasins or cutting stations. Then Dotty heard a hair dryer and footsteps above her and she realised the salon must be on the first floor.

"I …" Dotty paused, unsure how to continue.

"I've seen you before." The woman narrowed her eyes. "You're not a reporter, are you?"

"Oh no," Dotty reassured her. "But I was at Charbury Castle Hotel on Saturday. With the police." Or at least with Keya, who was a police officer.

"Then you know Natalie's been arrested, which is ridiculous."

"But it must have been a shock to find out her husband was cheating on her."

The woman examined her perfectly manicured nails painted with yellow varnish. "Not exactly. We suspected he was seeing someone else after I spotted him at Cheltenham Railway Station, just before Christmas, greeting a younger woman. I don't know why Natalie didn't kick him out. I don't think she could be bothered."

"But I heard her on Sunday," protested Dotty. "And she threw some choice language at Keely."

"Is that the name of his bit on the side?" The woman wriggled her fingers and looked at Dotty. "I guess it was the shock of finally meeting … Keely."

She spoke Keely's name as if she'd bitten a sour apple. "And it was stupid and disrespectful of Roger to bring her to an event so close to home. I don't think Natalie minded what happened when he went away, but at an event she attended, in front of her friends. That was a different matter."

Dotty heard footsteps and two women appeared behind the

reception desk. One patted her neat grey curls and the other, wearing a grey hoodie with a pink scissor logo over the breast pocket, said, "Julie will make you another appointment for six weeks' time."

She turned and Dotty noticed the pink scissor logo was also on the back of her hoodie. It reminded Dotty of something, but she wasn't sure what.

"Excuse me," said the woman behind the reception desk. She disappeared into an alcove and returned holding a fawn raincoat.

"Here you are, Mrs Robinson."

Dotty left the hair salon and retraced her route through Cirencester to the police station. As she was approaching it, her phone pinged, and she checked the message.

"Still in meetings. Come up to the office." It was from Aunt Beanie.

Dotty smiled. This was her excuse to find out what was happening with Natalie.

Only an overweight man, with a black and tan terrier curled up on the floor beside him, was in the police reception area.

Dotty approached the Perspex screen and the elderly officer acknowledged, "Bernadette told me to expect you. I'll just call PC Jenkins."

Dotty stood waiting, and after several minutes, the young police officer opened the door and handed her a lanyard.

As he once again led her up the concrete stairs to the first floor, she asked, "I heard Natalie Wright was arrested. Has Inspector Evans interviewed her?"

"Several times," the young policeman admitted, "But she's sticking to her story that she got in her car after her argument with Miss Clarke, and drove away from the hotel."

"And apart from a witness with dubious eyesight, there's no other evidence or reason to hold her."

PC Jenkins stopped at the stop of the stairs and turned to her. "I heard you've done this before. Detecting that is. And you're right. The inspector is furious that he can't find any other evidence to detain her. He's stalking around downstairs, snapping at everyone. That's why I've taken refuge upstairs. And they always have biscuits."

Dotty smiled as the tall young police officer led her to the Rural, Heritage and Wildlife Unit.

As she entered, she looked across to Chief Inspector Ringrose's corner office. He glanced in her direction and Aunt Beanie turned in her seat. She got up and walked across to open the office door, and called, "Help yourself to tea. I'll try not to be too long."

Dotty found the kettle and Yorkshire tea bags and made herself a mug of tea. PC Jenkins was right, there was a plastic container holding assorted biscuits.

She removed a shortbread finger and took it and her mug across to the desk where the young police officer was standing.

"What are you doing?" she asked.

"Trying to piece together the scraps of paper I found in that glass bowl on Roger Dewhirst's stall. But they're tiny."

"Shall I take a look?" Dotty asked.

"Be my guest." PC Jenkins stepped aside.

Dotty bit into her shortbread finger as she stared down at the tiny fragments of paper. One with a printed number on it caught her eye.

She put her mug and the rest of the biscuit down and picked up the piece of paper. "See if you can find any more with numbers like this printed on them."

They gathered together pieces of paper.

"This one has written numbers on it," said the police constable.

"Then start a new pile."

"Ok, let's see what we have." Dotty spread the numbered scraps out. "This one is a corner." She put it to one side, "and the rest are mostly edge pieces." She put them in a line.

PC Jenkins moved around the scraps with the hand-written numbers on. "2,000.00," he exclaimed.

Dotty looked from her paper jigsaw to the constable's and considered, "I think it's a cheque." Let's look for letters and see if we can find any names.

Their progress was slow, although they quickly worked out the cheque had been issued by Barclays Bank. The signature was difficult to read, but they found several pieces which they pieced together to form Roger Dewhirst's name.

"So the deceased wrote this cheque," mused Dotty.

"Maybe he made a mistake and tore it up?"

"But he was selling at the antique fair, not buying."

PC Jenkin's round boyish face frowned, but he quickly brightened as his finger slid another scrap away from the remaining pile. "Here's part of a name. Oli. That's a man's name."

"Not necessarily," countered Dotty, moving another scrap across to join it. "Olivia."

They found other scraps until they had the name 'Olivia Hambleton'.

"Who do you think she is?" asked PC Jenkins.

"I don't know," replied Dotty. "But our victim, Roger Dewhirst, wrote a cheque to Olivia Hambleton for £2,000, and presumably one of them tore it up into tiny pieces."

"Why?" asked the young police constable, his eyes wide.

Dotty looked at him and replied, "That's the question."

CHAPTER NINETEEN

"No, I think that lamp's better on the side table," instructed Marion.

Dotty picked up a cream Regency style bone-inlaid lamp, with a faded walnut-brown shade, and positioned it on a mahogany side table.

Dotty had been relieved when Marion called her on Wednesday evening and told her David was away for a few days, so could she come and help with the auction.

"There are so many Lots," complained Marion. "I wonder if we can display some elsewhere, otherwise it'll be crammed full in here and there'll be no room for customers to view anything."

"How about moving this small sideboard and those two semi-circular tables to the reception area, and we could display the collection of shepherdess figurines on them?"

"Good idea. Norman," Marion called.

It was Friday morning and Dotty had spent it, and all of Thursday, moving furniture from the storeroom into the main auction house and, under Marion's precise eye, positioning pieces to create attractive displays.

But with so many items that they'd had to extend the sale into

Friday morning the following week, it was a struggle to give each item space for viewing.

"Why don't I ask Gilly if we can create a display in the corner of the antiques centre?" Dotty suggested. "Some of the less valuable pieces of furniture ..."

"And a few of the carpets and some floor lamps. Why have we so many of those for sale this month?" Marion raised her arms as she looked around the auction room.

"Is January always like this?" asked Dotty as Norman approached and together they lifted a small oak dresser.

"Where do you want it?" asked Norman.

"In the reception area," replied Dotty.

"Not always," Marion responded to Dotty's question. "But we have had two-day sales in January before. It's a combination of no sale, or only a small one, in December, and people having a clear out in the new year."

Half an hour later Marion declared, "Lunch time."

Gratefully, Dotty returned to the office and switched on the kettle. She removed her metal sandwich tin, with a picture of chickens on the top, but remembered it only contained a single sandwich.

She hadn't wanted to ruin her appetite before her afternoon tea with Keya, but all the physical work this morning had made her hungry.

She sat on the spare chair and ate her thin ham sandwich and drank a welcome cup of tea while she chatted to Marion about the upcoming auction.

"I've been discussing our roles in this month's auction with George, and we wondered if you'd like to swap roles with me and sit up on the rostrum," suggested Marion.

Dotty's eyes widened. "Really. With George? I'm not sure about that."

"She'll be fine. Besides, now she's excitedly planning her trip to Paris she seems far less anxious and uptight than she has been for a while."

"But you know how she gets on auction days."

"I do," agreed Marion, stabbing the salad in her Tupperware

container. "But why not give it a go? I'll run through everything with you on Wednesday, once the computers and screen have been set up."

After lunch, Dotty and Norman moved two more tables and four chairs into the reception area.

"That's enough," instructed Marion, "But it looks good here. I don't know why we haven't utilised this space before."

Dotty found the box of porcelain shepherdesses and carefully unwrapped each figurine, arranging them on the shelves of the dresser or on one of the tables beside it.

The door from the antiques centre opened and Aunt Beanie walked in. There was a spring in her step and her red headscarf had been tied with a particularly large bow.

"I love preparing for auction day," admitted Aunt Beanie. "And it must be a busy sale if Norman is arranging furniture in the antiques centre."

"It's running into Friday morning," confirmed Marion.

"Which, allowing for delays, means you should be finished by mid-afternoon. You'll all be shattered by Friday evening. I'll ask George if she wants any help."

A second figure followed Aunt Beanie in from the antiques centre. It was PC Jenkins.

"Ryan gave me a lift from the station," disclosed Aunt Beanie.

"Ryan?" Dotty saw colour rise in the young constable's cheeks. "Oh, I see. Is this your first visit to Akemans, Constable?"

"It is. But I wasn't expecting it to be so busy," he replied.

"Always like this in the lead up to an auction," announced Aunt Beanie, "and especially January when people start spring cleaning and decluttering."

Dotty unwrapped brown paper revealing a young-looking shepherdess cradling a lamb under one arm and holding a crook, which was taller than the shepherdess in the other hand. Dotty was amazed it was still in one piece.

Aunt Beanie was bouncing from one foot to another.

"Is there something you want to tell me?" asked Dotty as she placed the figurine on a semi-circular mahogany table.

"Ryan and I have been discussing the case on the way here."

Ryan averted his eyes guiltily.

"Well, I am employed by the police," retorted Aunt Beanie.

"I know," appeased Dotty. "But I'm not."

"Oh."

Dotty giggled. "But I still want to know."

Aunt Beanie stepped closer and whispered loudly, "Sergeant Unwin oversaw another search of Roger's collection of, let's call them curios, and he discovered cash hidden away. Lots of it."

Dotty was about to reach for the final wrapped figurine, but she stopped and stared at Aunt Beanie. "Really! Where did that come from?"

"Nobody's really sure, are they, Ryan?"

The young constable joined them and, although he picked at the corner of his black jacket, he confided, "There were bundles of notes. When I last heard, they'd counted at least £20,000."

"Perhaps he was saving up to leave Natalie and start a new life with Keely," considered Dotty. "I assumed he'd been lying to her and had no intention of leaving his wife, but maybe I was wrong."

"Is £20,000 enough to start a new life?" mused Aunt Beanie.

"I think there was more money," replied Ryan.

Dotty unwrapped the last package, which was a shepherdess protecting her lamb from a snarling wolf. "But was it enough to kill for?"

CHAPTER TWENTY

After finishing her display of porcelain shepherdesses, Dotty collected her bag and coat and said goodbye to Marion.

Ryan, PC Jenkins, had made his excuses and returned to the station, although he'd seemed disappointed to be missing out on Keya's afternoon tea.

Dotty drove Aunt Beanie north to Hilcot Manor.

"I've heard the restaurant in the hotel is excellent, although expensive," said Aunt Beanie as they drove between two stone pillars with what looked like stone boiled eggs in stone eggcups on top of them.

Dotty decided that she must be hungry if inanimate objects were starting to resemble food. Her tummy rumbled.

Aunt Beanie must have heard as she remarked, "Didn't eat much lunch? Neither did I, and now I'm famished."

They followed signs to the cookery school, taking a right fork away from the hotel whose attractive stone proportions Dotty had only glimpsed.

They passed a large vegetable garden with several rows of canes tied into x-shapes. The only vegetables Dotty recognised growing were the tops of large leeks and a patch of round cabbages, although there were several other sections of green leaves.

The drive swept round to the left and, between it and a moss-covered stone wall, was a collection of raised beds.

Dotty recognised rosemary bushes and a clump of thyme plants, but she wasn't sure what was growing under the glass-topped raised beds.

The cookery school was housed in a converted traditional single-storey Cotswold stone barn with a sloping grey-slate roof. It was large, being some forty metres in length.

The gabled front entrance was a third of the way along, and as they arrived, Keya came running out. She was wearing a white apron with what Dotty presumed was the cookery school's logo and a huge, beaming smile.

"You made it!" she exclaimed.

"Of course," replied Aunt Beanie, climbing out of Dotty's Skoda. "Neither of us ate much for lunch and we're famished."

"You can't rush the ceremony," warned Keya. "You need to take your time savouring each morsel and sip of tea and, of course, enjoying the company."

Keya accompanied them through the glass-fronted entrance and, turning right, she led them between immaculate marble-topped work benches and gleaming stainless-steel ovens under the barn's exposed wooden rafters.

The kitchen ended and gave way to open plan space, filled with small square tables covered in white cloths. The room was light and airy and Dotty turned around to see large glass panels in wooden frames which she thought must slide open during the summer months.

There was a stone-flagged terrace outside and beyond, a typical Cotswold view of sloping fields, brown hedges and skeletal woods. It would be wonderful in the summer.

"Let me introduce you to our teacher," enthused Keya.

"Instructor, please," corrected a well-spoken, but warm voice. A lady with her long blonde hair tied back in a ponytail turned to greet them. She held out her hand and said, "Olivia Hambleton."

Dotty froze.

Wrinkling her forehead as she glanced at Dotty, Aunt Beanie shook Olivia's outstretched hand. "Bernadette Devereux and Dotty Sayers. We're so excited to be Keya's guests."

"And she's done a fantastic job making huge progress and even working on meat products for the first time. One of my top students," praised Olivia.

Keya's smile widened, and her eyes shone with pride.

"Excuse me," said Olivia, and she moved away to greet a couple being escorted by a teenage girl.

Aunt Beanie nudged Dotty. "What's got into you? Have you seen a ghost?"

Dotty shivered. "Sort of, but let's sit down."

The tables were filling up around them with chattering couples and proud cookery students.

When everyone was seated, Olivia Hambleton stood at the front of the room, with her back to the kitchen, and announced, "Welcome to Hilcot Manor Cookery School. Let me say how proud I am of all the students this week. I know they've worked really hard to prepare your afternoon tea. Please feel free to ask them any questions you have about the food, or choices of tea, and I'm here to help if they get stuck. Please enjoy."

Everyone clapped as the students stood up and moved into the kitchen. As Aunt Beanie picked up a handwritten menu, she asked, "So what made you lose your voice and your manners when we met Keya's instructor?"

"Olivia Hambleton. That's the name on the cheque that PC Jenkins - Ryan - and I pieced together on Wednesday when I was waiting for you."

Keya returned with two full chrome cake stands decorated with sprigs of herbs, which she placed proudly on the table. "I've written on the menu what everything is, but there are sandwiches, a sausage roll and a miniature salmon and dill tart on the bottom. On the middle plate, there are two scones, one plain and one with dried fruit, together with clotted cream and homemade raspberry jam."

Dotty's stomach gurgled, and she giggled.

Aunt Beanie gave her a stern look.

"And on the top there's a miniature strawberry tart, a chocolate brownie, a shortbread and lavender biscuit and," she looked up at Dotty, "a lemon flavoured madeline."

"Bravo," cried Aunt Beanie.

"It does look wonderful. Perhaps too good to eat," admitted Dotty.

"Before you do eat, you both need to choose your tea. I've written out the selection of teas and a little about them."

Dotty and Aunt Beanie both looked at their menus.

"I'll try the Darjeeling," said Dotty.

"With milk or lemon?"

"Oh. I think I'll stick to milk."

"I'll have the Earl Grey, with milk," said Aunt Beanie.

Keya left, and Dotty reached forward for a sandwich.

Aunt Beanie grabbed her hand and chided, "Wait for Keya. Besides, I want to get a photo first. Can you take one?"

Dotty removed her phone from her bag and took several shots of the cake stands, and when Keya returned, one of her with Aunt Beanie and another on her own with the cake stand and a pot of tea.

Keya made one more trip to the kitchen before finally returning with a smaller cake stand which she placed in front of her own place setting.

"Can we start now?" asked Dotty as Keya removed her apron and sat down.

"Of course," replied her friend, still smiling proudly.

Aunt Beanie poured tea into a delicate china cup decorated with blue and yellow flowers. She took a sip and in a satisfied tone said, "That's what I needed."

Dotty bit into her sausage roll. The pastry was light and buttery, and the filling flavoured with sage and apple." She closed her eyes, savouring the taste.

Keya laughed. "You really were hungry?"

Dotty nodded, finishing her mouthful. "Starving. Norman and I have been moving furniture all day to Marion's exacting standards."

Next, Dotty tried a coronation chicken sandwich with a tang of apricot.

Aunt Beanie leaned forward and said, "Dotty wants to ask you about your instructor."

"Why? Do you want to come on a course? She's very professional, and patient. It took me ages to master sausage rolls," admitted Keya.

Dotty shook her head. "It's not about food." She lowered her voice. "You know you instructed Ryan," Keya drew her eyebrows together,

"PC Jenkins, to bag those scraps of paper he found in a glass bowl on Roger Dewhirst's stall?"

"Yes," replied Keya in an uncertain tone.

"Well, we pieced the bits together on Wednesday and they were from a cheque. One written by Roger to Olivia Hambleton for £2,000."

"What?" Keya's hand shook and tea splashed down the side of her cup.

Aunt Beanie handed her a white linen napkin to mop it up.

"Why would Roger give her a cheque? And who tore it up?" asked Keya.

Dotty reached for a cheddar and onion chutney finger sandwich and replied, "That's what we need to find out."

CHAPTER TWENTY-ONE

"Has Norman left already?" asked Dotty sleepily on Sunday morning as she entered the kitchen at Meadowbank Farm. Aunt Beanie was already sitting at the pine table reading the Sunday papers.

"Yes, I heard the Land Rover start up just after half past seven, but I checked the animals and they're happy, so Norman must have fed them."

Earl Grey meowed as he twisted around Dotty's feet. She pulled the chrome kettle off the hot plate and remarked playfully, "And I doubt he was allowed to leave before you'd been fed."

Aunt Beanie said, "I bought some bacon and mushrooms while I was out, and there are some sausages in the fridge. What do you think about a full English breakfast before I leave for church?"

"That sounds great. But what about Norman?" Dotty poured her tea.

"I made him some sandwiches last night, and left him some soup to heat up and put in a flask for when he finished. He's hoping to walk all morning. Are you still OK picking him up?"

"Of course." Dotty wasn't sure what else she was going to do for the day, except chauffeur Norman back to his car after he'd finished his walk.

Aunt Beanie chuckled. "Why don't you have a shower and wake up while I start on breakfast?"

Dotty carried her mug of tea back to her cottage and did as Aunt Beanie had suggested. She returned to the farmhouse kitchen twenty minutes later, her hair still damp in places.

The smell of caramelising sausages greeted her, and so did Earl Grey as he once again twisted around her legs. "You'd like a second breakfast, would you?"

Earl Grey looked up at her and meowed.

"Make yourself a fresh cup of tea and sit down," suggested Aunt Beanie. "I'm nearly finished. Your friend Ozzie Winters has written another disparaging piece for one of the Sunday papers, which I think will interest you."

"She's not my friend," retorted Dotty, but she sat down at the kitchen table and slid the open newspaper towards her. The article was shorter and the headline smaller than the previous week, but it was still an achievement for a young journalist to have a follow-up piece published.

The headline proclaimed, 'Murder Suspect Released', and Dotty read with interest that a disgruntled - that was a polite way of putting it - Inspector Evans was forced to release Natalie Wright on Friday afternoon due to lack of evidence.

Aunt Beanie placed the tomato ketchup and knives and forks on the table and asked, "Do you think the inspector did the right thing, letting the wife go?"

"I doubt he had any choice. He'd arrested her on the evidence of a witness with questionable eyesight, who thought she'd spotted Natalie arguing with her husband after she told the police she'd left. I don't think they've found anything to actually link Natalie to the toasting fork or Roger's death. Have you heard anything?"

"No," replied Aunt Beanie as she placed a large plate of scrambled eggs on toast, two sausages, two rashers of bacon, several baked cherry tomatoes and a spoonful of fried mushrooms in front of Dotty.

"I didn't hear any updates on Thursday when I was at the station, but we did make some progress with the stolen jug. Not good news, I'm afraid. The chief inspector reached out to some of his contacts and one of them thought he'd seen the jug being packed for shipping, but the consignment had already left."

"Did he know where it was going?"

Aunt Beanie sat down and mumbled a prayer to herself.

Dotty caught the word Cliff. Aunt Beanie had been to visit Uncle Cliff the previous day and said he was content in the care home, but Dotty knew she was upset that he was struggling to recognise her.

"Sorry, what did you say?" asked the older woman.

"Does the chief inspector's contact know where the jug was being shipped?"

"Belgium. But that doesn't mean anything. It's the European centre for antique smuggling and counterfeits. The jug could be sent anywhere from there."

"And the contact had no idea where?"

"None, or at least if he did, he wasn't telling the chief inspector. But it does tell us one thing," mused Aunt Beanie.

"That Ernie realised too late that it wasn't a twentieth century reproduction, and it was valuable."

"He'll be kicking himself." Aunt Beanie cut the end off a sausage and popped it into her mouth.

Just as they were finishing, Dotty's phone rang.

"Norman?" enquired Aunt Beanie. "He's not been as long as I expected."

"No, Keya," replied Dotty, as she answered the call.

"Hiya," greeted Keya. "What you're doing today? I haven't much in the fridge, and I've heard of a farm shop north of Cirencester, just off the A417 near Duntisbourne Leer, that serves a buffet afternoon tea. I thought it might be fun to try it out, as part of my research."

Dotty wasn't sure what Keya was researching. Afternoon teas, she presumed.

"When were you thinking? I have to pick Norman up around lunchtime."

"Two o'clock? I'll meet you there as I'm popping into work this morning. The chief inspector wants me to look through foreign news reports and social media. He's trying to track the copper jug stolen from the fair."

"Aunt Beanie's just been telling me about it."

"I'll see you later, then."

Dotty was in her cottage, reading the book she'd bought on collecting pottery and porcelain, when her phone rang.

"Dotty," Norman shouted down the phone. Wherever he was, it was noisy, with what sounded like traffic.

Dotty lost the next couple of words. "Sorry Norman, what did you say?"

"I'm at the Air Balloon pub, at Birdlip. On the roundabout."

"I know the one. Wow, you've walked far. Give me five minutes and I'll be on my way."

"Thank you. I'm going inside for a pint."

Dotty checked on Earl Grey and found him curled up on her bed. She stroked him and said, "I'll see you later."

Her cat purred but made no effort to move.

She drove north along the dual carriageway section of the A417, past the turning to Duntisbourne Leer, where she spotted a sign with a pink pig directing customers to Piglet's Farm Shop, where she was to meet Keya later.

The Air Balloon was hard to miss, positioned halfway down the Cotswold escarpment, beside a roundabout where traffic either continued west towards the M5 motorway, turned towards the northern edge of the attractive spa town of Cheltenham, or headed into the Cotswolds.

Dotty found Norman inside, finishing a pint of beer.

"That's just what I needed. And I had a bacon sandwich while I waited. But don't tell Beanie, as she made me some sandwiches last night."

They walked out to Dotty's car and Norman placed his muddy rucksack in the back. "I'll be pleased to take my walking boots off," admitted Norman as he climbed into the car.

"Where to?" asked Dotty.

"Charbury Castle Hotel, or at least the small car park next to it."

"I didn't know there was a car park near the hotel," said Dotty as she checked her phone for directions. It took her through

Duntisbourne Leer. At least it wouldn't take her long to get back to the farm shop to meet Keya. It was already half-past one.

As they approached the hotel Norman said, "See the track on the right?"

"Yes."

"Drop me at the entrance. I've stiffened up and need a walk before I can drive."

Dotty did as directed. As Norman climbed out and collected his rucksack, Dotty glanced down the rutted track and spotted the farm's Land Rover Defender at the end.

"See you back at the farm," called Norman, as he closed the car door.

Dotty continued to stare down the track, wondering about its proximity to the hotel.

CHAPTER TWENTY-TWO

Dotty entered Piglet's Farm Shop and stopped to gaze around. Along one wall, wicker baskets and wooden crates displayed healthy looking fresh vegetables.

On the other side, a butcher stood behind a fresh meat and deli counter serving customers. Throughout the shop, shelves and racks were laden with delicious looking food items including sauces, cakes, and chutneys.

She was tempted to stop and browse, but thought she'd better check if Keya had arrived.

"Hiya," called Keya, standing up and waving from halfway down the cafe. She'd done well to secure a table, as every other one was full.

"Have you been here long?" asked Dotty.

"Half an hour. A constable at the station warned me there'd be a queue at lunch time. I've only just sat down, and now I'm starving. I think it must be the smell of homemade leek and potato soup."

"Is that what you're having?" asked Dotty.

"No, I've come for the vegetarian afternoon tea selection. Apparently we're given two plates, one for savoury treats and one for sweet, and we can choose five items from each section. The food is supposed to be delicious." Keya grinned excitedly.

Dotty looked down at the menu. "And a large choice of teas."

"I thought I'd try the lapsang souchong, which is a black tea from China," enthused Keya.

"Then I might try the Ceylon tea from Sri Lanka," said Dotty, caught up in Keya's eagerness.

Keya chose a cheese and chive quiche, a vegetarian scotch egg, a cheese straw, and two sandwiches, one with Wiltshire mature cheddar and farmhouse pickle and the other with trout pâté and cucumber.

Dotty also chose a trout pâté sandwich and, as it was Sunday, a roast beef and horseradish one. She added a sausage roll and a selection of cubes of cheese with crackers and spicy tomato chutney.

"Did you track down the missing jug?" asked Dotty.

Keya shook her head. "No. I couldn't find a trace of it. But I'll keep looking. Mind you, I didn't get much time to search as my email box was full of messages from my favourite village."

"Lemington? What's happened? Has someone cut a neighbour's tree down or scratched a car?"

"No, in fact, it's amazing. The villagers are united this time, against a new property owner."

Dotty nodded in understanding as she chewed a cracker with a wonderful smokey cheese and hint of chilli from the chutney.

Keya leaned closer and disclosed, "An Arab gentleman has bought the hall, and the inhabitants aren't happy."

"I see. But they can't expect you to do anything about it."

"I know," groaned Keya. "But they still like making a fuss." She bit into her quiche and a dreamy look crossed her face. "Amazing."

Keya finished chewing and said, "Did you hear Inspector Evans had to release Natalie Wright? He was furious."

"I bet he was. But I've been thinking," confided Dotty. "Norman asked me to drop him off at a car park next to Charbury Castle Hotel. And it's made me wonder about Natalie's story."

"Can you access the hotel from it?"

"I'm not sure. I dropped Norman off at the top of the track."

"The hotel's not far from here. Why don't we have a look when we're finished?"

Dotty smiled in relief. "I hoped you'd say that."

"Paying for your own meal this time or expecting someone else to pick up the bill," asked a male voice with a sarcastic note.

Dotty stiffened, and Keya dropped her scotch egg back onto her plate.

They looked up to see Quinn, the young man who'd shared their table in The Orangery at Charbury Castle Hotel, frowning down at them.

"Oh, no!" cried Keya, as her hand shot up to cover her mouth.

"We didn't pay for lunch last Saturday, did we?" Dotty spoke slowly, as she remembered leaving Quinn and rushing after Keya. And she'd offered to pay for lunch.

"No, you didn't," replied Quinn.

Keya turned to Dotty and said, "We'll definitely go back there this afternoon and settle up."

"No need," said Quinn flatly. "I paid."

"Oh, thank you. How much do I owe you?" Dotty asked, removing her purse from her bag.

"Nothing." He rubbed his hands down his jeans. "Actually, I wondered if you could help me?"

"How?" asked Dotty.

He turned to Keya. "It's you, actually."

"Me?"

"Yes, you're a police officer, aren't you?"

"I am."

"Then I'd like you to speak to my parents. When you're finished."

"OK," Keya's response was hesitant. "Can I ask what it's about?"

"They've been robbed."

"Haven't they reported it?"

"It's not that simple. We're sitting over in the corner when you're ready. There are two extra chairs, so feel free to bring your sweet course." He finally managed a weak smile as he suggested, "And I recommend the macaroons."

Dotty watched Quinn weave around tables and join an elderly couple in the corner of the cafe, beside a window.

Keya leaned forward and hissed, "What was that all about?"

"Me forgetting to pay. Sorry, I hope it hasn't placed you in a difficult position."

CHAPTER TWENTY-THREE

Dotty and Keya carried their empty dessert plates across to a counter displaying the sweet selection of afternoon tea treats.

"I'm not sure how much I can eat," admitted Dotty, studying the array of beautiful tarts, pastries, biscuits, and cakes.

"Pick five anyway, and one of us can take home what you don't eat. This is research, after all," Keya reminded.

"Research for what?" Dotty picked up a slice of Bakewell tart and placed it on her plate.

"You know I said I didn't want to spend the rest of my life working for the police?"

"Yes." Dotty chose a pink macaroon, accepting Quinn's suggestion.

"Well, I think I've told you before that I'd love to open a cafe. I still would, and I think I can make it work around my police work to start with, particularly if I can reduce my hours."

"Which is why you took the baking course, and we're here today?"

Keya placed a strawberry tart on her plate. "Exactly. Now what else do you like the look of?"

"That curd tart is different, and the lemon and pistachio cannoli is attractive."

"It says that these Australian lamingtons are vegetarian. They're covered in coconut, but I've no idea what's in the middle. I think I'll try one." Keya placed a square morsel coated in white flakes of coconut on her plate.

Quinn joined them as they returned to their table. "I can't keep my parents here much longer. Can you come and speak to them now? I'll carry your teapots if you bring your cups?"

Dotty glanced across at her friend, guilty that their fun afternoon was being interrupted by work, and that it was her fault.

"OK," Keya agreed.

They allowed Quinn to lead them across the cafe to a table beside the window where a dignified older couple were sitting. Dotty suspected the table was meant for four people, but there were three empty chairs and she, Keya and Quinn, sat down, rather close to each other.

"Mum, Dad, I'd like to introduce you to some friends of mine," began Quinn.

But when he didn't give their names - did he even know their full names? - Keya leaned forward and said, "Hi, I'm Sergeant Varma, with Gloucestershire Police, and this is my friend and police consultant, Dotty Sayers."

Dotty noticed the older couple flinch when Keya gave her rank. Had Quinn told his parents Keya was a police officer? And was Keya making the conversation more official by elevating her to a consultant?

"Quinn told me you need to report a robbery," Keya said gently, but professionally.

Quinn's mother dabbed her eye with a lace-edged white handkerchief and his father gave Quinn an imploring look.

"Dad, you've lost £20,000. You're retired now and you need that money. These ladies might be able to help you. Besides, they were there when Roger Dewhirst was killed."

Dotty wrinkled her forehead. "Does this have something to do with Roger's death?"

"No," Quinn responded quickly. Too quickly? "Not unless he's duped other people out of their life savings," he added angrily.

Keya found space on the table to place her hands and suggested, "Shall we start at the beginning?"

Quinn took a deep breath, composing himself and looking at his father, he said, "Dad."

The older man straightened his tie. He looked Keya in the eye and introduced himself. "Jeremy Hughes, and my wife, Sarah." He glanced across at his wife, who closed her eyes and nodded.

"We first met Roger Dewhirst in a restaurant in Cheltenham. It's an expensive one, but we were treating ourselves to celebrate my retirement from an accountancy firm."

"He'd been there for thirty-five years," added Sarah Hughes, before once again dabbing her eyes with her handkerchief.

Her husband continued, "The gentleman at the table next to us was well presented, with a brown tweed waistcoat, the matching jacket thrown over a spare chair. He did speak a little loudly into his phone and I couldn't help overhearing parts of his conversation."

Quinn's father sipped from his glass of water. "He was talking about a property I knew, Hardingly Hall. I used to do the estate accounts until some big London firm wowed the old major, and he gave them his business. From what Roger Dewhirst was saying, I gathered the major had died and his estate was being sold off. That made sense. He had no children and his nephew had never been interested in the hall."

Dotty bit into her macaroon as Jeremy paused. Pink crumbs scattered across her plate.

Jeremy continued, "The gist of the conversation Roger was having - or pretending to have - was that he could buy the entire contents of the house at a heavy discount and sell off the pieces, one-by-one and make a decent profit. But time was of the essence.

"He said he could get his hands on £30,000, but the extra £20,000 he needed was tied up in longer-term investments. He asked the caller - real or otherwise - if he wanted to join the venture and invest the required £20,000. It seemed as if the caller was interested but needed to consider it further. I'm not sure how I got into a discussion with Roger ..."

"His jacket fell on the floor, don't you remember?" queried Sarah Hughes.

"You picked it up for him and mentioned that you'd overheard him saying the major was dead, and that you used to know him. The next minute Roger was sitting at our table and within ten minutes you'd agreed to invest £20,000 of your retirement money in his scheme." Sarah sounded bitter.

"But you didn't try to dissuade me," countered her husband.

"Would you have listened to me if I had?"

Jeremy rubbed his nose and admitted quietly, "Probably not."

Sarah drew her lips together in a thin line.

Dotty placed her cold cup of tea back on its saucer and said, "So you agreed to invest £20,000 in Roger's scheme to buy the contents of Hardingly Hall?"

Jeremy nodded.

"Except the old major isn't dead," disclosed Keya. "Unless it happened very recently. I saw him at a forestry conservation meeting at the beginning of the month."

Jeremy squeezed his eyes shut before admitting, "I found out later that he was away for the second half of last year, visiting friends in South Africa and he'd had an accident and broken his leg, which delayed his return. After the meeting with Roger in the restaurant, I visited Hardingly Hall and seeing the closed curtains and unkept garden, I presumed Roger was telling the truth.

"I'd seen inside the house and there were a couple of attractive paintings of gun dogs, and some nice landscapes. And from what I remembered, most of the furniture was a decent quality. So I met Roger and handed over £20,000 from my retirement fund. But after that, he stopped returning my calls. Even changed his number."

Sarah Hughes wrinkled her nose in a disapproving manner. "Disappeared with our money and we never saw him again."

CHAPTER TWENTY-FOUR

Sarah Hughes jumped up and, ignoring her chair which fell over, rushed out of the cafe at Piglet's Farm Shop. Jeremy carefully righted the chair and stood up himself, saying, "Excuse me," as he followed his wife.

Quinn broke the silence. "My parents are proud people, and my father is usually very careful. He's embarrassed to have lost so much money to a conman."

Quinn stood up but added, "I'm not sure if there is anything you can do to recover their money, but I do appreciate your help." He smiled weakly and left.

Dotty looked down at her plate. She'd half eaten her lemon and pistachio cannoli but hadn't touched her slice of Bakewell tart or her piece of oatie flapjack.

A young waitress approached them and placed two bills on the table. Dotty picked them up and realised one was for her and Keya, but the other was for Quinn and his family.

Had he deliberately left them to pay the bill? Or had he, like she and Keya the previous week, been distracted and genuinely forgotten about it?

Keya leaned across and read the bills. She snatched their one and said. "I'll pay this one. Are you OK picking up the Hughes bill? It's a bit cheeky asking for our help and leaving us to pay for their tea and scones."

Dotty checked the bill. It was for £28. "It's not too much. Probably similar to our own last week. Quid pro quo, I think the term is."

Keya widened her eyes. "If you say so."

Dotty waited for her change, which she gave back to the waitress as a tip as she took a brown paper bag from her, containing their left over cakes.

As they weaved their way between tables, many of which were now empty and had been wiped and set for their next occupants, Keya's phone buzzed.

"Hello," she said, answering it. "I'm with Dotty and we're just leaving Piglet's Farm Shop and heading to Charbury Castle Hotel to follow a hunch Dotty has."

She waited for the caller on the other end. "Sure, we'll meet you there, although we're actually interested in a small car park next to the hotel." Another short break and then Keya finished the call with, "See you soon."

As they walked out into the chilly air, Keya said, "That was Sergeant Unwin. He's going to meet us at the car park."

"Did he say why he wants to meet us on a Sunday afternoon?"

"No, just that he needed to speak to me."

Dotty led the way in her green Skoda and Keya followed in her much speedier Ford Focus.

She slowed as she drew closer to the hotel entrance, searching for the track where she'd dropped Norman earlier. She indicated and turned into it, but after ten metres she braked to a stop.

There were two large puddles in front of her, half-filled with water, and they looked deep. Too deep for her little car.

She climbed out and, stepping around other puddles, walked back to Keya who'd parked several metres behind her.

Keya wound down her front window and asked, "What's up?"

"I don't think my car will make it down this track. You can go past me and try if you like, but there are two huge puddles in front of me and I can't tell how deep they are."

Keya leaned out of the window.

There was still another fifty metres or so of track.

"I don't think I'll risk it." She looked behind her. "We'll have to reverse. There's nowhere to turn."

Carefully and steadily, Keya and Dotty reversed back to the road. They pulled onto the verge beside the entrance and climbed out of their cars as a metallic grey Mercedes appeared round a bend in the road.

It slowed down and pulled into the entrance. With the engine still running, Sergeant Unwin climbed out and said, "I thought we were meeting in a car park?"

"We were, but you need a 4x4 to reach it." Dotty pointed down the track. "Too many potholes, and some have water in which might be deep."

"But we can go on foot," suggested Keya, wrapping a long, multicoloured wool scarf around her neck.

Sergeant Unwin looked down at his pristine white trainers. "Not in these. Why the interest in a potholed track and empty car park?"

"I want to know if the car park can be reached from the hotel," replied Dotty.

Sergeant Unwin looked down the track and then along the road to the manicured hotel entrance. "Why don't I park at the hotel," he suggested, "and see if I can find the track and meet you at the car park, or halfway between the two."

"OK," nodded Dotty.

Keya grinned. "Leave us to do the dirty work."

Sergeant Unwin gave her a lopsided smile as he climbed back into his car and drove off.

"Come on," said Dotty. She was glad she was wearing her brown buckskin ankle boots, but she still didn't want to get them wet or too muddy.

"Just a minute," called Keya from the back of her car. She emerged wearing a pair of black rubber wellies.

"That's very organised of you," admitted Dotty.

"I keep spare clothes, a jacket, and various high-vis clothes and signs in my car," Keya explained. "All part of a policewoman's kit."

They picked their way along the track, stepping onto the long grass verge in places where there were too many puddles.

"What about Quinn and his parents?" asked Dotty. "Do you think they'll be able to get their money back?"

Keya hesitated and then stepped off the track and onto the edge of the neighbouring field, trying to avoid a large thistle. "Potentially, if Roger has enough money, but I doubt he has. He's probably spent it all by now."

Dotty followed her friend, squeezing between the thistle and a clump of nettles. "But what about all the cash?"

Keya stepped back onto the track but turned towards Dotty and asked, "What cash?"

"PC Jenkins said that during another search of the items Roger sells at fairs, the police discovered large amounts of cash. He said there was at least £20,000."

Keya walked on, considering, "What if Quinn heard the money had been discovered, or he's in some way connected to Roger or his wife and already knew about it? He and his parents, if that's who they are, might have made up this whole story. Maybe they're the ones trying to con us."

"You don't really believe that, do you?" queried Dotty. "Sarah Hughes would have to be an impressive actress. She seemed genuinely embarrassed, upset, and annoyed, all at the same time."

"And her husband told a detailed story. It did ring true, but I'll still check them out, just to be sure before I go round demanding their money back."

They reached a small car park, nearly as muddy and potholed as the track. But there were a couple of wooden picnic tables on a grassy bank at the front and a fantastic view over the valley beyond.

"I bet this is a lovely, secluded spot in summer," observed Dotty.

"But not somewhere to hang around in winter."

"Sergeant Varma, can you hear me?" Sergeant Unwin called.

Keya walked across to the edge of the car park and looked across at the trees, which appeared to mark the hotel boundary. "Yes, I can hear you. Where are you?"

"I've found a faint path along the boundary wall. Hopefully, there'll be a gate or something."

"Look," Dotty pointed to a narrow winding path where the grass was shorter than the rest of the field.

"We'll come and meet you," Keya called back.

She led them along the path. It was nothing like as bad as the track, but they still had to step over or around several shallow-looking muddy puddles.

"I'm through," called Sergeant Unwin, and he appeared at the edge of the trees, to their right.

The path turned in his direction and the sergeant started walking towards them. "I found an old kissing gate in a gap in the wall," he called. He halted and swore, looking down.

Keya turned to Dotty and giggled. "I don't think his trainers are white any longer." Turning back to Sergeant Unwin, she called, "Wait there. We'll come to you."

A minute later, they were with the sergeant.

Dotty asked, "Was the path easy to find?"

"I had to retrace my steps. The main path comes from the back of the hotel, along part of the drive, and then down past The Orangery. There is a signpost, mostly hidden in a tree, where the path forks. The main path goes to the back of the hotel grounds and there's a stile over a fence into a field, where it disappears down the valley. This is the smaller path leading from the fork to the car park you found."

Sergeant Unwin stepped back, allowing Dotty to navigate the kissing gate. She pushed the narrow gate away from her, stepped into the gap at the widest point of the semi-circular fence surrounding it, and swung the gate past her, stepping out the other side.

As Keya followed her manoeuvres, Sergeant Unwin asked, "So why are the car park and track important?"

Dotty watched him enter the kissing gate and asked, "What if Natalie did drive away from the hotel but was also at it?"

Keya frowned. "That doesn't make sense. She couldn't be in two places at once."

"No, not at the same time," clarified Dotty. "But what if the witness did see Natalie arguing with her husband?"

"She didn't." Sergeant Unwin shook his head as he led them along a narrow path between large trees, bare without their leaves.

"Didn't what?" asked Dotty.

Sergeant Unwin explained, "The witness didn't see Roger and his wife arguing. The blonde-haired woman was called Olivia Hambleton."

"My baking instructor!" exclaimed Keya.

Sergeant Unwin stepped into a small clearing and looked back at Keya. "Yes, which is why I wanted to speak to you about her."

"Of course, the cheque." Keya turned to Dotty. "You said you'd pieced together the scraps of paper from the stall and that it was a cheque the deceased wrote to Olivia."

"Correct," confirmed Sergeant Unwin. "Which is why I've been trying to pin her down for questioning and finally managed to interview her this morning."

Dotty asked, "What was her explanation?"

Sergeant Unwin looked around. "Let's walk back to the hotel and grab a drink."

They all agreed, and Dotty and Keya followed him back along a wider, gravelled path. Dotty stopped and peered through a window into The Orangery. It was closed, and tables and chairs were stacked up beside the stone wall at the back.

She was certain she'd seen something important when she'd been sitting inside with Keya.

In the hotel bar, Sergeant Unwin ordered half a pint of beer, but Keya and Dotty stuck to tea. "I need something hot," Keya said, blowing on her hands.

The bar was relatively empty, and Keya and Dotty sat on the red velvet bench which ran along the wall while Sergeant Unwin pulled out a stool and sat down, placing his glass on a round beer mat, with a picture of a man's bearded face, on top of the circular table.

"Olivia Hambleton," began Sergeant Unwin, "claims that last November she sold Roger Dewhirst an attractive Okra glass bowl. He offered her £2,000, and she was delighted. He wrote out a cheque and two weeks later, she took it to the bank and deposited it. But the cheque bounced, and the bank told her the account had been closed."

The barman brought across Keya and Dotty's tea.

Sergeant Unwin sipped his beer. When the barman retreated, he continued, "Olivia didn't see Roger again, but she went to the antique fair last Saturday specifically to speak to him. But when she confronted him, he denied he'd done anything wrong.

"He told Olivia it was her fault for not cashing the cheque sooner. She argued that a two-week delay was not unusual, and that he should honour their deal and pay her what he owed. He refused, and in her anger and frustration, she tore the cheque up in front of him. Apparently, he watched her nonplussed, gathered the pieces together and put them in a bowl."

"Which is where PC Jenkins found them," concluded Keya.

"Did Olivia confirm when she had her argument with Roger?" asked Dotty.

"Late morning, she said, before she met her husband in the restaurant for lunch. And that is why I don't believe Natalie was in the marquee arguing with her husband."

Dotty felt deflated. "I really thought I was onto something."

Sergeant Unwin placed a hand on her arm and consoled her. "It was an excellent piece of detective work."

She smiled back at him.

CHAPTER TWENTY-FIVE

The change in atmosphere at Akemans on Monday morning was palatable. It was auction week and with the sale continuing into Friday, rather than just the usual one-day sale on Thursday, everyone was feeling under pressure.

Dotty was first to arrive at eight o'clock, and she let herself in by the auction house's front door, which was normally kept locked for security reasons. But during an auction week, such as this, it was unlocked, making it easier for staff and visitors to access the building.

Dotty settled herself at the spare office desk to check her emails. She didn't want to move any of the papers and personal items Marion had left on the main reception desk, which faced the front door.

There were a few emails about items being entered into February's auction and someone asking for a list of auction dates. Why didn't they check the website? She'd posted the dates of all the year's auctions when she returned to work at the beginning of January.

There was also an email about an antique fair in a country house in Worcestershire the coming weekend. Had she had enough of antique fairs? And yet … she'd speak to Keya.

She stood up and went to the kitchenette at the back of the small office, turning on the white kettle.

"Morning," called Marion as she stepped through the front door.

"Are you ready for a busy week?" Marion removed her black wool coat and cream scarf and hung them on the coat stand in the corner of the reception area, beside the door which led into the antiques centre.

Underneath, she wore a pair of tailored black trousers with a green floral blouse and short black cardigan. A gold necklace with green stones hung around her neck. Dotty wasn't sure if Marion wore costume jewellery or the real thing, but she suspected the latter and that David sourced it during his trips.

"Is David back?" asked Dotty.

"Detained. He hopes to be home tonight so he can help us tomorrow evening at the first viewing. Which means," Marion removed two transparent Tupperware boxes from her bag and moved towards Dotty, who was still waiting for the kettle to boil, "that you and I should run through your auction duties while things are still relatively calm and quiet."

Marion placed her containers in the small undercounter fridge, next to Dotty's own metal sandwich tin with chickens on.

Marion reached up to a cupboard and removed a container of her special coffee, as Dotty made her tea, and asked, "Can you find the company tablet?"

Dotty found the tablet and sat down at her desk with it and her tea.

Marion pulled her chair across to Dotty's desk and began, "On auction day you will have two screens," she explained. "The main one will display TheAuctionRoom.com website, which we use as our reference, and George will read the description of each item from it. But you also have to watch a second online site, BidatAuction.com. I've no idea why we have to use two sites. It would be so much easier with one, but that's not my choice."

Marion made it sound as if she'd make changes if it was. She continued, "I'll make sure both sites are linked to our own system, so that when bids are placed on the internet, or you manually make the change from a bid in the room or on the telephone, everything will simultaneously update. Mind you, BidatAuction.com often lags behind and you have to wait for it.

"What we tend to do is open the bidding and let the internet do its thing. Once it stops, you'll need to see what proxy bids you have. Make sure you print yourself a list of those on Thursday and Friday morning, as I'll be snowed under issuing bidding numbers. We start from zero for the January auction and everyone has to resubmit their details."

Dotty realised just how busy the upcoming auction was going to be.

Marion continued, "So once the internet stops, check the proxy bids and show George if there are any above the current bid, and then she'll open the bidding up to the floor. It won't be easy to spot people with so much furniture in the room, so you'll have to be alert and keep checking to see if a new bidder has raised their hand. As you know, it's not always obvious. Sometimes just a nod of the head or a slight raising of an auction brochure."

Dotty's head was spinning. There was a lot of responsibility helping George and with so many things to check, she could easily make a mistake.

Marion was watching her and her face softened. In a reassuring tone, she said quietly, "I know I'm making it sound complicated, but there is a system and I'm sure you'll soon get the hang of it."

She slid a green sheet across the desk. "The final thing you have to do is fill this in. The bidder number goes here, and the winning bid here, and do you remember the codes we use?"

Dotty nodded her head. At least she was familiar with the green sheets, as it was usually her job to enter the information from them onto the computer system which generated the invoices.

"Good." Marion stood up. "Let's finish setting up the auction room."

Norman and Dotty worked hard, moving more furniture and large auction pieces in the morning and after lunch, they started in the smaller auction room, at the far end of the main one.

Metal racks were attached to three walls, on which Norman hung paintings and pictures, while Marion arranged jewellery and more valuable silver and gold items in lockable glass cases running along the fourth wall.

Dotty was unwrapping crystal glasses, which were part of a sizeable set, and placing them on a table when Aunt Beanie appeared carry her blue and white striped basket.

"It's taking shape in here," she announced. "That's an attractive swan," she said as Marion removed bubble wrap from a table centrepiece, about thirty centimetres in length.

Marion held it up. "And solid sliver, but I'm not sure how many people still host dinner parties and want such impressive pieces for their tables."

"Enough," replied Aunt Beanie. "While others like to display them in cabinets. Personally, I think they take too much cleaning."

Sergeant Unwin stood in the doorway. "I hadn't realised how much work it takes to set up an auction." He moved across to the table where Dotty was arranging glasses and picked up a wine glass. "We could have a great party with these."

"You'd need a quality wine to drink out of them," commented Norman, hanging up a painting of two cows beside a tree. One was lying down while the second stood behind it, looking directly at the painter. "Not cheap supermarket plonk."

Marion placed the silver swan in the cabinet and countered, "But I expect those glasses, which are quality crystal ones, will be cheaper at Thursday's auction than most new, plain glasses."

Aunt Beanie joined Dotty and picked up a heavy-bottomed tumbler.

"Have you been to the office?" Dotty asked her.

"Yes. Chief Inspector Ringrose called us all in, as he's still trying to locate the stolen copper jug from the antique fair."

"And have you found it?"

"Keya used a method she called keyword searches, and she found this." Aunt Beanie reached into her basket and removed a folded piece of paper.

Dotty unfolded it and her attention was immediately drawn to a photograph of the jug she'd seen on Ernie's stand at the fair at Bath Showground.

"It was unveiled in Iraqi's National Museum," explained Sergeant Unwin.

Dotty mumbled, "Now there's a surprise," as she scanned the newspaper article.

"Why do you say that?" asked the sergeant in a confused tone.

Dotty looked up and replied, "Because it's not the first, or even second item, I've personally seen in the Cotswolds, which has ended up in that museum."

"Which is where it clearly belongs," reasoned Marion, opening a small, flat green leather case.

Dotty wrinkled her nose. "I know there are those, like David, who think so. But this item was stolen."

Marion placed the open case, which contained a beautiful gold necklace with a teardrop-shaped emerald surrounded by diamonds, in a display case. "Exactly, and now it's been returned."

CHAPTER TWENTY-SIX

"Keya sends her apologies," said Aunt Beanie, placing a cut-glass tumbler back on the table beside the collection of glasses Dotty was arranging in the smaller auction room.

"But Chief Inspector Ringrose wanted a full debrief on the copper jug." She looked sideways at Dotty as she added, "So Sergeant Unwin kindly offered me a lift, as he wants a word with you."

Dotty did not look up or meet Aunt Beanie's questioning gaze.

"I only need to take your statement from your meeting with Quinn Hughes," the sergeant explained.

"Which one?" asked Dotty as she placed the final glass on the table and stepped away, considering how best to present the collection.

"How many have you had?"

"Keya, Sergeant Varma, and I first met Quinn on the day of the antique sale at Charbury Castle Hotel, and we spoke to him and his parents yesterday at the Piglet's Farm Shop cafe."

"It's yesterday's meeting I'm most interested in. Is there somewhere we can talk? In private?"

"Give me two minutes." Dotty moved the glasses around until they were arranged in rows in size order. Satisfied, she said to Sergeant Unwin, "Let's go back to the office. I need a cup of tea."

"Norman, tea?" asked Marion.

"I wouldn't say no," replied Norman.

"Neither would I," proclaimed Aunt Beanie.

"Dotty, can you make tea for us all and Norman or I will come through and collect it in a moment?"

Back in the office-cum-reception area, Dotty said to Sergeant Unwin, "Why don't you sit down while I make everyone drinks."

The young sergeant was flicking through the auction catalogue when Dotty approached the grey sofa and tub chairs in the corner of the reception. She placed his mug of coffee on the reclaimed-elm table and sat down clutching her own mug of tea. "So what would you like to know?" she asked.

"Just tell me your version of yesterday's discussion with the Hughes and I'll write it down," instructed Sergeant Unwin.

When Dotty had finished, Sergeant Unwin asked, "And you think they were telling the truth?"

"Yes, Mrs Hughes was genuinely upset. Why, don't you?"

"I do. In fact, we found Roger's diary and an entry at the end of October mentioning '20K' and the initials 'JH'."

"That corresponds with their story, although they waited a long time to tell the police. It would have been much easier to sort this out with Roger Dewhirst still alive."

"Maybe they were trying to sort it out privately, without the police's involvement, but now Roger is dead, they have no choice but to come to us."

Dotty sipped her tea, thoughtfully. "Why was Quinn at the antique fair? Do you think he went to find Roger Dewhirst? Or perhaps he knew Roger was going to be there and wanted to confront him. Yet another person who had a bone to pick with Roger that day."

"Are you suggesting Quinn had something to do with Roger's death?" asked Sergeant Unwin, placing his notepad and pencil on the table and picking up his coffee mug.

"It's possible. He arrived at our table less than ten minutes before Edith and Ethel burst into The Orangery and announced Roger was dead. He would need to be a cool customer though, as he was relaxed and composed when he asked to sit with us. Mind you, he did have a shocked expression on his face when Keya announced she was a police officer."

Sergeant Unwin drank his coffee, staring over Dotty's shoulder. Finally, he said, "I see what you mean. If he and his parents had been trying to track Roger down for the last couple of months and he'd been ignoring their calls ..."

Dotty interjected, "Jeremy Hughes said Roger changed his number after initially refusing to answer their telephone calls."

"So the only way they could try to get their money back was to approach him in person."

Dotty drummed her fingertips on the tabletop. "I remember now. Quinn said he was staying with his parents to sort out some problem they were having and that he doesn't actually live round here."

"I need to run a check on Quinn Hughes. Anything else I should know?" asked Sergeant Unwin.

"If Quinn was only staying with his parents to help get their money back, and Roger was proving elusive, he might have become frustrated. Or perhaps he'd already approached Roger, at another fair, and Roger had refused to return the money, making Quinn angry."

"Angry enough to kill you mean?"

Dotty raised her eyebrows. "I don't think we can rule him out."

Dotty waited for Sergeant Unwin to stand, but instead, he picked up his notebook and consulted it. Looking up, he caught Dotty's eye and remarked, "You said Quinn was yet another person with a bone to pick with Roger. Who were the others?"

"Apart from his wife and girlfriend, whose reasons are obvious, there was Olivia Hambleton with the bounced cheque, and a young man called Billy, who Roger refused to do business with, and Ethel and Edith, who complained that he hadn't paid them for the scam which they run at fairs."

"What scam?"

"They see a customer who's interested in a particular, usually high-value item, but doesn't buy. They agree with the stallholder that if the customer returns and purchases the item for a certain amount, they get a cut of the sale. They're colourful old ladies, probably trying to make a few extra pounds, and it doesn't really hurt anyone."

"But how do they persuade the customer to buy?"

"Keya calls it FOMO. The ..."

"Yes, I know what FOMO means, and I think I understand. Worried that someone else will grab a bargain, the customer returns to buy it." Sergeant Unwin nodded his head.

What had he bought because he thought he was missing out? His flash car, perhaps?

Sergeant Unwin cleared his throat and asked, "Any idea where I can find this Ethel and Edith, or the other man you mentioned, Billy, was it?"

"No, but there's another antique fair this weekend. They might be there. I was going to ask Keya if she wanted to go, but would you be interested?"

"Definitely. I need to get my head around how they work. Where is it?"

"Near Malvern, in Worcestershire."

"I'll drive us there and we can make a day of it. On duty, of course. Do you think there'll be somewhere nice to eat?"

"Who knows? But you might solve the case before the weekend."

Sergeant Unwin's shoulders sagged. "I doubt it."

CHAPTER TWENTY-SEVEN

The rest of the week flew by, taken up by auction viewings on Tuesday evening and all day Wednesday, and the auction itself, which didn't finish, as Aunt Beanie had predicted, until mid-afternoon on Friday.

George had insisted on pushing on without a break for lunch on Friday, so everyone was exhausted by the end, and hungry.

David had arrived back for the viewing on Tuesday evening and was a great help at the auction, organising the telephone bids and assisting Dotty by spotting bidders in the room.

They'd only missed one, a woman hidden from them behind a standard lamp with a large lampshade, but she called out as the hammer fell and they allowed her to bid. She bought an attractive quality pair of deep red curtains for the bargain price of £45.

On Saturday morning, Dotty dragged herself out of bed at half past seven. She'd have preferred a lie-in and a lazy day, but she'd promised to go to the antique fair near Malvern with Sergeant Unwin - who'd asked her to drop the formalities and call him Nick - and Keya.

Dotty thought Keya didn't want to miss out on the fun, FOMO again, but then she'd explained that Jay Newton had set a date for his charity tabletop sale. He'd asked her to organise it, so she needed to research how to set up and run one.

Both Aunt Beanie and Norman were sitting at the pine table in the farmhouse kitchen when Dotty entered. She was dressed in jeans and calf-high suede boots, with sheepskin at the top, and a grey jumper and scarf.

"Grab yourself a cup of tea. The kettle's just boiled," instructed Aunt Beanie. "Norman's been telling me all about the auction. I hear you did an excellent job assisting George. Before we know it, you'll be auctioneering."

Dotty felt her face flush. "I don't think so, but I did learn a lot from George, and I can understand why she gets so worked up before an auction. You have to concentrate all the time on the bids from the internet, on the books, the phone, and the room. And I agree with Marion. I can't see the point of two online bidding platforms. It'd be so much easier with just one."

At the table, Norman yawned.

"You should tell George that," suggested Aunt Beanie.

"I doubt she'd listen to me." Dotty placed a slice of brown seeded bread in the toaster and sipped her tea.

Earl Grey appeared and rubbed himself against her legs.

"There is one advantage helping George, and that's being in the thick of the auction," admitted Dotty.

"In the office, I always feel I'm missing out on the action. And from the rostrum, when bids are opened up to those in the room, I can watch people's faces and see their reactions. Some are clearly organised, with notes written on their catalogues and they've worked out the commission and the top price they're willing to pay, while others bid on a whim."

"And then they complain afterwards that they've paid too much and why does Akemans need so much commission? Do they think we're a charity?" asked Norman.

He looked shattered and his eyes were red. He'd worked really hard all week, first moving items into place to show them off before the auction, and then during and after the bidding as he helped carry items to purchasers' cars and vans.

"It was exciting watching the bidding on popular items. That silver tabletop swan you saw Marion with," Dotty looked at Aunt Beanie as she heard the toaster pop signalling her toast was ready, "sold for over £6,000."

She started to butter her toast as she added, "and the gold necklace with the emerald and diamond teardrop sold for just over £4,000."

"Excellent," agreed Aunt Beanie. "But why the rush this morning? Is that young sergeant taking you out?"

"Nick?"

"On first-name terms, are we?"

Dotty felt the blood rush to her cheeks. "It's just less formal than calling him Sergeant Unwin all the time and not very practical today, although it is a work trip. We're going to an antique fair near Malvern, and Keya's coming too."

Dotty heard a car horn.

"That'll be them now. I'm not sure when I'll be back." She took a last gulp of tea, and grabbed her toast, her blue padded coat and a small brown shoulder bag. She stopped to stroke Earl Grey. "Behave yourself," she told him before dashing out of the farmhouse.

Keya was already in the back of Nick's metallic grey Mercedes. She looked a little cramped.

"Are you alright in there?" asked Dotty, before shoving the last of her toast into her mouth.

"I'm OK, and I can always stretch out if I need more room."

"Don't put your feet on my leather seats," chided Nick.

Keya giggled.

It was infectious, and Dotty smiled as she slid into the car. It was going to be a fun day.

As they reached the dual carriageway of the A417, Dotty glanced across at Nick and asked, "Do you have a plan for the day?"

"Not really," he replied. "I'm interested in getting a feel for a fair and how they work, so I can try to understand why nobody saw the murder weapon being taken, or Roger Dewhirst being killed. And I'd like you to point out some of the regulars, and characters like Billy and the two old ladies."

Dotty asked, "Are you going to question them today, at the fair?"

She watched him pucker his lips before replying, "I'm not sure. I'll see how it plays out. But I'm not convinced that someone like Billy will give me his true contact details, and he is likely to vanish until the next fair."

"I think you're right about that," agreed Keya from the back.

Their conversation led them away from antique fairs to other gossip from the police station. As they drove through a small village, past a pond and a pub called the Red Lion, Dotty asked, "How are your unruly villagers, Keya?"

"Unbelievable. Because the purchaser of the hall is a foreign gentleman, they think the police have the power to block the sale. I keep telling them we live in a free market and if someone from the Middle East thinks their village is attractive enough to live in, then perhaps they should welcome him. I explained that he was unlikely to be in residence all year, but if they treated him well, and included him in village life, he could be a generous benefactor."

"And how did that go down?" asked Dotty.

"The only person left at the end of my speech was an old woman who wanted me to fix the door on her garden shed."

Dotty laughed at Keya's comical expression in the driver's mirror.

"I think this is it," Nick said as the post and rail fence on their left gave way to a stone wall and they spotted a sign for the antique fair which told them it was being held on the Friday, Saturday and Sunday.

"What if we've missed all the bargains, and there's nothing left today?" cried Keya.

"I very much doubt it. Besides, what are you looking to buy?" asked Dotty, swivelling around in her seat.

"Things," muttered Keya, before biting her lip.

They turned into the gravel drive of a well-proportioned Georgian-style house, not dissimilar to Windrush Hall except the stone was lighter. There were steps leading up to the entrance, flanked on either side by stone columns, and four large casement windows occupied each side wing.

Nick was directed to park beside the entrance steps, near a vintage silver Mercedes.

He smiled proudly as he climbed out, looking up towards the front door. "I could get used to this."

"The entrance to the fair is over here," called Keya as she strode towards a single-storey building, set apart from the main house.

Dotty was disappointed. She'd wanted to look round the main house.

CHAPTER TWENTY-EIGHT

Inside the smaller building, a smartly dressed man in a tweed suit said, "Three people. That'll be £18."

"I have this," said Keya, handing over a sheet of paper, "But I'm not sure if it's still valid."

The man peered at it through his wire-rimmed glasses. "A voucher from our website, absolutely, so two for the price of one and an extra person is £12."

"I'll pay," Nick said. "And can I have a receipt?"

As the man sorted out change and handed Nick three thin catalogues and his receipt, Dotty sniffed the air.

"There's a cafe behind me, selling drinks and homemade snacks," explained the man.

Dotty could smell a deep rich soup, with chicken and vegetables, she thought.

Keya moved towards the cafe entrance, but Dotty caught her arm. "Later. Let's have a look around first."

Nick was already moving towards the first stall, which had books arranged on a table and the shelves resting on it.

Dotty was surprised. They seemed to be entering a corridor and moving away from the single-storey building.

"The stalls are in the basement, ground and first floor of the house, and you're free to look around the rooms which are open on those floors," called the man from the reception desk.

The lady standing beside the bookstall, where Dotty stopped, told her, "The house is only open to the public during antique fairs and a Christmas fair they hold here."

Dotty looked at Keya, who smiled back. A Christmas fair was their type of event.

Between stalls, there was a gas heater behind a makeshift metal fence, made from what looked like a fire guard. Keya held her hands above it before they moved on.

They must be entering the basement. The floor was smooth grey concrete and the stone walls were painted white. As they turned the corner, Dotty noted doors leading off the main corridor and a line of servants' bells high up on the wall.

She imagined in the past, family members in the main house above pulling a rope in the room they occupied, say the drawing room, which would be attached to a particular bell. The servants would have known immediately where they needed to go.

The first room they entered had paintings displayed on one side and old framed maps on the other. The paintings were not hung on the walls of the room but on green baize partitions which formed secondary internal walls.

Keya bent over to peer at the written description of two large oil paintings in fancy gilt frames. Each depicted a spaniel sitting down with a game bird, which Dotty presumed had just been shot by its master. Not a subject she'd like on her walls.

"£16,500," quoted Keya. She stood up and examined the paintings and, mirroring Dotty's thoughts, pronounced, "I wouldn't want them in my house."

Nick was flicking through a pile of maps of Gloucestershire.

"It's a smarter fair than the one at Charbury Castle Hotel," commented Keya. "I hope our suspects are here."

They left the basement, climbing the concrete stairs to the ground floor.

"This is more like it," enthused Keya, as she stared up at the ceiling.

Dotty also looked up and examined the fancy plaster cornicing with gilt highlights. They were at one end of a long corridor, which opened out into a gallery. The rooms on either side of her were not occupied by stalls. She stepped into one.

It was a library, and she slowly circled a central table, reading the titles of some of the books arranged along the walls. There was a complete set of Encyclopaedia Britannica, and three volumes of the History of Worcestershire.

On another wall, tall, green, leather-bound books had their contents printed in gold lettering on their spines. One was for Rents 1878, and another was Accounts 1884. There were no computers back then, and the estate belonging to a house like this could have been large.

She glanced up at a painting of a young man hanging above the fireplace. A label, which was part of the frame, told her it was Viscount Upton in 1934.

Keya poked her head round the door. "It looks like more of our regular antique fair stalls are on this floor. I'm going to speak to some stallholders and see if I can find out more about the stolen copper jug."

Dotty followed her out into the corridor, but her attention was caught by a man ducking into a doorway just ahead of her. She thought it was David and followed him into the room.

Inside partitions of green baize walls had created a large stall, occupying half the room, which was set up like a shop. Heavy oak furniture was positioned around the edges, interspersed with smaller mahogany and rosewood pieces.

Bronze statues of birds and horses were displayed on the furniture, along with enamelled trinket boxes, glass vases and gilded mantel clocks.

She stepped closer to one wall where a gold and purple brocade chapan hung from the wall. The label said it was silk, and it certainly looked fine and colourful.

Not unlike the ones she'd seen at Gainfords' auction, although, if anything, it looked more impressive. Even the buttons were embroidered. A lady approached the stallholder and engaged her in conversation. There was no sign of David.

"Dotty, are you coming?" called Nick from the doorway.

She had a last look around, frowning, before joining Nick in the corridor.

"Right, let's see if we can find Billy and the old ladies," announced Nick in a businesslike tone.

They walked between rows of smaller stalls selling a variety of objects, but Dotty thought there was more quality and less bric-a-brac than usual.

Ernie was there with his stall of copper and brass items, which shone in the light thrown by overhead chandeliers. Keya was talking to him but she detached herself and asked them, "Did you see Ethel, or was it Edith, heading in your direction? Like last time, she was wearing yellow."

Nick shook his head.

"Sorry, I was caught up looking around the library and one of the stalls," Dotty admitted. "Was she on her own?"

"Yes," replied Keya.

"Probably just answering a call of nature," suggested Nick. "Let's keep moving."

Nick and Dotty left Keya, who returned to speak to Ernie, and walked slowly down the corridor.

Suddenly, Dotty grabbed Nick's arm and whispered, "That's Billy. Over there, with the short, dark, wispy hair. Let's move closer so we can hear what he's saying."

Dotty and Nick edged closer to Billy, stopping at a jewellery stall. Dotty pretended to examine a pair of bird-shaped brooches as she listened to Billy and the stallholder next door.

Billy picked up a modern, rectangular-shaped vase with splashes of green and yellow running through the otherwise clear glass.

"How much for this, luv?" he asked.

"£30."

Billy frowned as he examined the vase. "Not worth much more than £15, surely."

"£25," replied the stallholder.

Billy pulled two ten-pound notes out of a back pocket of his jeans. "£20 for cash?" he asked.

The woman on the stall wrinkled her brow before replying. "Go on. Do you want it wrapped?"

"No. I'll just carry it, thanks." Billy moved away.

Dotty whispered. "That's the first part of Billy's act. Buying a piece."

"Would you like me to take the kingfisher and swan brooches out of the case so you can see them close up?" asked the lady at the jewellery stall, her heavily ringed hand rested on the glass display cabinet.

Dotty smiled at her and replied, "Not at the moment, thank you." She turned to Nick and said, "Let's follow Billy."

Keya, who was talking with another stallholder, saw them and stepped into line as they walked quickly down the corridor.

Billy entered a room at the far end.

They followed.

This room did not contain green baize partitions, and it felt opulent with golden-yellow papered walls, an ornate ceiling, and heavy gold curtains hanging above two large windows.

The stalls in the room were small and most sold jewellery, but Billy had approached one at the far end, by the marble fireplace, with a deep-blue velvet table covering and lighting which illuminated an attractive display of glassware.

They didn't hear Billy's conversation with the stallholder, but the transaction was quickly completed and Billy pocketed at least ten twenty-pound notes.

Nick leaned towards Dotty and whispered in her ear, "Not a bad day's work."

He looked around the room and suggested, "Let's speak to him while he's in a good mood. Dotty, can you hang back and cover the door we came through, in case he makes an escape? And, Keya, can you stand in that doorway, which leads to an adjacent room?"

Keya and Dotty acknowledged his instructions by moving into position. Billy had turned away from the glass stall and Nick confronted him in the middle of the room.

Dotty saw Billy's eyes widen and quickly search for escape routes.

Keya stared back at him from the doorway where she stood, arms folded across her chest.

Nick held his hands up in a conciliatory gesture. "Don't worry, Billy, I'm not about to arrest you for that deal you've just done. Tidy profit, by the way."

Billy pursed his lips and his eyes still flitted to the doorways.

"I only want to ask you a few questions about Roger Dewhirst."

So Nick had decided to question Billy at the fair, rather than waiting until the following week.

"What about him?" asked Billy. He tried to sound defiant, but a tremor betrayed his nervousness.

"Perhaps you'd prefer to speak somewhere more private. How about I buy you a coffee in the cafe downstairs?"

"All right," replied Billy as he stepped around Nick.

Nick gripped Billy's arm and walked with him towards the entrance door where Dotty was standing. She heard him say, "Just a precaution."

CHAPTER TWENTY-NINE

Dotty was about to follow Nick and Billy when Keya joined her and said, "You go with Nick. I'm going to keep asking questions around here."

"Don't you want a cup of tea?" asked Dotty.

"And a piece of chocolate cake." Keya's eyes momentarily glazed over. "When I'm finished," she said resolutely.

Dotty descended the concrete stairs to the basement and followed the corridor back to the entrance.

She caught up with Nick and Billy as they entered the makeshift cafe. The serving area was a cloth-covered table, and two more tables set up in the corner formed the kitchen area. There was still a mouth-watering smell of chicken soup.

As they sat down on mismatched wooden chairs around a square table, Billy gave Dotty a sly look and asked, "Haven't I seen you before, with David Rook?"

Dotty hooked her brown bag over the back of her chair before turning to face Billy. "I work with David at Akemans."

Billy nodded, giving her a knowing looking.

She wrinkled her brow uncertainly.

Nick cleared his throat as an elderly woman appeared and said,

"You need to order at the front. It isn't table service." She turned on her heels and returned to the serving table.

Nick looked at Billy and then across to Dotty and raised his eyebrows.

Taking the hint, Dotty said, "I'll get these. Billy?"

"Coke."

"Strong black coffee, please," requested Nick, his eyes not leaving Billy.

Dotty order the drinks at the serving table, hoping she wouldn't miss out on the interview, but Nick and Billy remained silent. More customers entered, chatting happily.

"Here's your Coke, and your coffee." The woman placed a can and mug on the table. "I'll just get your tea."

Dotty carried all the drinks back to her table and, as she sat down, Billy pulled back the ring pull on his can and glugged the contents.

Nick cleared his throat again and started, "Billy, a witness saw you arguing with Roger Dewhirst shortly before he was found dead at the Cotswold Antique Fair."

Billy spluttered, and Dotty wondered if he'd inhaled bubbles.

"Grumpy …." Dotty lost the rest of the sentence as a man scraped a chair along the concrete floor behind her.

Billy continued, "Not my fault he doesn't know a quality item when it's on his own stand, staring him in the face. I bought a Rudolf Schrotter vase from him, fair and square. I may have bid him down from his £20 asking price, but that's to be expected."

Dotty leaned forward and said, "But you told him it was a fake."

"I didn't, actually. I only asked him a few questions. Besides, he'd hardly be asking £20 for it if he thought it was genuine."

"And I bet you made a nice few pounds selling it on," remarked Nick.

Billy stuck out his chest as he replied, "I did, as it happens."

"But Roger was refusing to do business with you again," reasoned Dotty.

"Oh, Roger was like that. And he's not the only stallholder who takes the hump after feeling I've ripped them off. But it's only business, my business, and most of them know that and come round in the end."

"And Roger?" asked Nick.

"Another couple of weeks and we'd have had a beer together and all would have been forgotten. Shame someone had to do for him. I've had some good pickings over the last couple of years."

"And you're sure Roger would have come round this time? Or was there something else which the two of you had fallen out about?" asked Nick.

Billy shuffled uncomfortably in his seat as he mumbled, "I don't know what you mean."

Nick pressed, "Did Roger say or do something that upset you?"

Billy remained silent, staring at his empty can of Coke.

"Something which made you so angry you stabbed him?"

Billy's eyes bulged and his mouth fell open. He looked genuinely shocked. "Now hold on just a minute." He jumped up, knocking over his chair and sprinted out of the cafe.

Dotty made to stand, but Nick placed a hand on her arm. "Let him go. I won't get any more information out of him today. Besides," he removed a transparent bag from his black jeans pocket, "we now have his fingerprints, so on Monday I can learn exactly who Billy is. I guarantee his prints will be on our system."

Nick placed the empty Coke can in the bag and frowned.

"Shall I carry it for you?" Dotty unhooked her brown bag. There wasn't a lot of extra space, but she removed her phone and pushed it into her jean's pocket, making room for the plastic bag and Coke can.

Nick finished his coffee and as he placed his mug back on the table, he asked, "Now, what about these old ladies of yours?"

"They should be easy to spot, if they're both wearing yellow."

Dotty and Nick checked the rooms in the basement, but there was no sign of Ethel or Edith. They climbed the concrete stairs to the ground floor and spotted Keya talking to a lady with white curly hair who was wearing a yellow jacket and trousers.

"Looks like Keya has done our work for us," Nick observed.

As they approached the pair, they heard the older lady implore, "But I've no idea where she is."

"Calm down, Edith. Look, here are my colleagues. They'll help look for her. Why don't you go downstairs and have a cup of tea?" suggested Keya, placing her hand on Edith's arm.

The older lady flinched and pulled away. "I don't want tea. I want my friend."

"Mrs ?" asked Nick in a voice of concerned authority.

"Miss, but everyone calls me Edith." Edith gulped and grasped her walking stick, planting it firmly in front of her.

"When did you last see your friend?" asked Nick.

"About an hour ago. She said she had to do something and rushed off along the corridor." Edith pointed back towards the stairs Dotty and Nick had just climbed.

An hour ago meant she hadn't seen Ethel since Keya had spotted her, when she'd been speaking to Ernie, the stallholder.

"What if she's stuck, or she's fallen over and hurt herself?" cried Edith.

"That's why we need to look for her," replied Nick calmly. He turned to Keya, lowered his voice and asked, "Is there anyone who can stay with her? It's a large house, and I am concerned about Ethel. We all need to look for her."

"Just a minute." Keya trotted down the stalls and stopped by Ernie's. She said something to him and then he accompanied her back along the gallery.

Ernie put a comforting arm around Edith and, as he led her away, he said, "Let's leave the police to look for Ethel. You come and sit with me."

Nick watched her go before turning to Dotty and Keya. "We had a quick look round the basement just now, so let's leave that until last."

"I'll go upstairs," volunteered Keya. "I haven't been up there."

"I'll start in the library and work my way along the rooms leading off the gallery," suggested Dotty.

"Good," agreed Nick. "And I'll start in the front entrance hall."

Dotty entered the library again. There wasn't really anywhere to hide, apart from under the table, but there was no old lady concealed there.

The room opposite the library was a drawing room. She reached out to touch the gold wallpaper.

"Don't touch that," an authoritative female voice said. "It's pure silk."

"Wow," responded Dotty, drawing her hand back. "It must have cost a fortune."

"It certainly did."

The woman, who had a name badge pinned to her black jumper and carried a radio, looked official.

Dotty asked, "Have you been here all morning?"

"I have. I move to the first floor after my lunch break to work the lift."

"And have you seen an old lady wearing a yellow?"

The woman smiled and replied, "She wandered in about half an hour ago looking for her friend."

"That must have been Edith. Was she wearing trousers and a jacket, and did she have curly hair?"

"Yes, that's the one."

"Is she the only older lady you've seen wearing yellow?"

"Yes, how many of them are there?"

"Two," replied Dotty, "And like Edith said, we've lost her friend Ethel. Can you keep an eye out for her?"

"Of course, but I go for my lunch in ten minutes."

Dotty moved down the gallery and entered the room she thought she'd seen David enter earlier. There were half a dozen people in the stall - the antique fair must be getting busier - but no sign of Ethel.

The stall only filled half the room, so Dotty walked through a gap between the end of the baize partition and the room's marble fireplace. She froze. Although the curtains were drawn, the yellow-clad figure of Ethel was impossible to miss.

CHAPTER THIRTY

Ethel was half-lying, half-sitting on an expensive looking creamy-gold sofa which went so well with her outfit and her scarf. A scarf which was wrapped around her neck and covered her mouth.

Her face was grey and her bloodshot eyes stared unseeingly at Dotty.

Ethel was dead.

Dotty backed out of the room and into the stall. Should she clear it? How could she? She had no authority.

She turned quickly and strode out of the room and along the gallery, her boots padding softly on the marble floor. Up ahead, she saw Nick walk out of one room and continue along the gallery, away from her. She started to run, feeling surprised eyes upon her.

As if sensing a change in atmosphere, Nick stopped and spun round. He caught Dotty as she stumbled into him and he whispered, "What's the matter?"

She blurted, "I've found Ethel."

With his hand behind her back, Nick guided her along the gallery. People stopped talking and watched them. Dotty's legs felt as if they would buckle beneath her.

Keya ran down the marble stairs from the first floor and when she reached them she blurted, "Have you found her?"

"In here," murmured Dotty as she led Nick and Keya past the stall and through the gap between the baize partition and the fireplace.

She hadn't been mistaken. Ethel was still slumped half on and half off the sofa.

"Heart attack?" asked Dotty, as Keya approached the body.

Dotty remained standing by the fireplace, but Nick followed Keya. He took several photographs with his phone before nodding at Keya who unwrapped the scarf, revealing the lower portion of Ethel's face and her neck.

A neck with several bruises and a clear red line.

Keya turned and exclaimed, wide-eyed, "She's been strangled!"

Businesslike, Nick addressed Keya by her police title and instructed, "Sergeant Varma, can you close the door to this room and interview everyone in the stall, particularly the owner, who might have seen Ethel enter … and her killer leave?"

Keya spun on her heels, and Dotty heard a large door slam shut.

As voices called, "Hey, what are you doing?" Nick turned to Dotty.

"Can you go downstairs and tell the man at the entrance that there's been a police incident, and that nobody is to leave or enter, apart from the authorities, until I give the go ahead? Is that clear?"

Dotty nodded.

His voice softened as he added, "Then get yourself a cup of sweet tea. You can leave this to me and Keya. You're in shock. It's never pleasant finding a body, even if the person is elderly."

Dotty leaned against the banister as she made her way to the basement. Her legs still felt weak. As she approached the entrance, she saw several people waiting and then spotted the queue outside.

She approached the man with the tweed jacket and wire-rimmed glasses and said, "I'm sorry, nobody else can come in."

He glanced at her quizzically and returned to his work.

Dotty took a deep breath. Time to pull herself together. She pushed past the group of people paying and closed the entrance door.

"What are you doing?" the man with the wire-rimmed glasses exclaimed.

"There's been an incident upstairs. The police are aware and already at the scene, but they've asked that nobody enters or leaves without their authority. An ambulance will be on its way, and there may be more police."

Dotty heard people muttering and one gentleman asked, "What kind of incident?"

A shriller woman's voice called, "Is anyone hurt?"

Dotty refused to answer their questions. She also refused Nick's suggestion of a cup of tea and instead turned and pushed her way through the gathering crowd, back along the basement corridor and up the concrete stairs.

As she reached the ground floor, she saw Edith push open the large door into the room where Ethel was. Dotty ran to catch up with her, which she only did as Edith collapsed on the floor beside the sofa. Beside her friend.

Nick stood with his back to the room, speaking on his phone. He turned as Dotty appeared, and his eyes widened as he spotted Edith.

Dotty leaned over Edith and took hold of her arm, pulling her up. "I'm so sorry, but you'll have to keep your distance."

"But she's my friend. My only friend," blurted Edith. "What happened? Who did this to her? We never meant any harm."

Edith felt like a dead weight and Dotty half-carried, half-dragged her to a creamy-gold chair which matched the sofa. Tears poured down the old woman's wrinkled face.

Dotty squatted beside her, and Edith placed her hand on Dotty's. It felt cold and paper-like.

In a surprisingly strong voice, Edith said, "Promise me you'll find out who did this?"

"That's a job for the police," replied Dotty sympathetically, "but I'll help in any way I can."

Nick joined them and asked, "What connection did Ethel have to Roger Dewhirst?"

"Roger! Surely you don't think their deaths are linked? That they were both …" Edith could not bring herself to complete the sentence.

"Until we have the results of the autopsy, we're exploring all possibilities. Now you and Ethel made a bit of money at these fairs, didn't you?"

"Yes, but there was no harm in it."

"Any disgruntled customers or angry stallholders?" pressed Nick.

"We just nudged some customers to buy items they were already interested in. And even if stallholders had to give us a cut of their profits, a sale is a sale in this business. And any stallholder who didn't want to work with us just had to say. We never did anything without first agreeing terms with them."

Dotty was half-listening to the conversation as she wondered why Ethel had left Edith earlier in the morning. She asked, "Could Ethel have been involved in something else without your knowledge?"

"I suppose so. She was the driving force. I only came along for the ride. It's far more interesting than my daily life."

"Do you know if she was meeting someone today? If that's why she left you earlier?" asked Nick.

Edith gave him a lopsided smile. "I've no idea."

Nick scratched his chin. "Worcestershire Police are on their way." He beckoned to Dotty, and as she joined him in the corner of the room, he whispered. "They'll want to interview Edith again, but I'm not sure what else she can tell them at the moment. And she looks exhausted. Why don't you take my car and drive her home?"

He held out the keys to his Mercedes.

"Me? Drive your car?" Dotty knew Nick treasured his car, and it was so powerful, unlike her little Skoda.

"Just treat her gently, and don't slam you foot on the accelerator. But be careful, she does eighty without even trying."

"Shall I come back for you and Keya?"

"No, I've called PC Jenkins, and he's coming over with a squad car. I'm hoping that Worcestershire Police will be occupied with the body and the young constable can start questioning people at the fair. See if they saw anything we missed."

Dotty took the keys and helped Edith to her feet. "I'll take you home while we leave the police to their work, so they can find out what happened to Ethel."

"I'll escort you out." Nick led the way down the gallery as Dotty followed more slowly, helping Edith. They turned right into the main marble-clad entrance hall.

As Nick spoke to a man wearing a badge and carrying a radio, Dotty glanced around. A figure ducked behind a pillar beside a stall selling glass and porcelain.

Was it Keely? Roger's girlfriend.

The man with the radio opened the front door and Dotty helped Edith down the front steps and into Nick's car.

She turned the ignition key, and the engine purred into life. Driving carefully away from the main house, she pulled over to let an ambulance pass before turning right out of the gates. In her rear-view mirror, she saw a police car approaching from the opposite direction.

"Where to, Edith?"

"Burford."

CHAPTER THIRTY-ONE

As Dotty slowly pressed the accelerator of Nick's Mercedes, she said, "Burford's lovely, although I guess it gets busy in the summer with all the tourists."

Beside her, Edith replied, "I suppose so. I rarely get a chance to go into town."

"Did you and Ethel live together?"

"Oh no! I never visited Ethel's house. She wouldn't take me." Edith looked down at her hands, clasped together in her lap. "I think she was embarrassed."

"Really, why?" Dotty braked a little too hard and she and Edith's heads shot forward, their bodies restrained by their seat belts. "Sorry, it's the first time I've driven this car."

Edith didn't seem to notice, as she replied, "I had the impression Ethel lived on her own. I'm not sure she ever married. She was very independent and drove herself everywhere. She always picked me up, pretending to be my younger sister."

"And you didn't mind that?"

"Why should I? It got me out. But she did mention something about Gloucester once, and how nice it was for me living in the countryside."

They joined the M5 motorway, heading south, and Dotty pressed her foot down on the accelerator. The Mercedes shot forward. She eased off the pressure as she asked, "Had you known each other long?"

"About ten years. We met at a garden open day in early summer. I'd left the rest of my group, who were slowed down by wheelchairs and walking frames, and wandered through the gardens to some small local stalls. I spotted Ethel stealing a packet of something from the cake stall. At the time I thought it very daring, but in hindsight, I don't think she could afford to pay for it. We sat down on a bench and she shared her swag with me. Millionaire's shortbread. It was delicious."

Dotty slowed down and indicated to leave the motorway.

"We talked and discussed our lonely lives. Then she mentioned she'd seen a poster at the entrance to the garden advertising an antique fair and wondered if I'd be interested in going to the fair with her. So I did. I paid for the entrance, of course, and the petrol, and lunch. But I didn't mind.

"The scam started as a bet with a stallholder who was disappointed an American gentleman hadn't bought a painting. Ethel, always up for a challenge and a way to make money, bet him that if the gentleman returned and paid a particular amount for the painting, the stallholder would give her £500. That was a lot of money to Ethel. We were discussing the painting when we realised the American gentleman was listening. When we met his eye, he turned on his heels, went back to the stall and bought the painting. Just like that. Which is how our little business started. And it was fun."

As the road climbed up the Cotswold escarpment, Edith stared out of the car window. Dotty heard her murmur. "Such fun. But tiring."

"What was that?" asked Dotty.

"Ethel had so much energy. She'd always wanted to do just one more, when all I wanted to do was sit down with a cup of tea. So sometimes she worked without me. I'm not sure how, but she'd come back grinning, a handful of notes clasped in her hand."

"Is that what happened this morning? Do you think Ethel went off to do her own thing?"

"I'm not sure. She was anxious, but also excited. And she'd started talking about a holiday. One of those package types to somewhere far too hot."

"So you think she was working something bigger? Something more risky?"

"I just don't know," replied Edith in an exasperated voice. "I wish I did."

They reached the roundabout at the top of Burford and Dotty indicated left. "Where do I go now?" she asked.

"Follow the road down the hill and turn right before the bridge. The care home is along that road, on the left."

"Burford Care Home?" Dotty asked in surprise.

"Yes," replied Edith, sighing.

Dotty waited for the wooden gates to open and then parked on the gravel drive. The raised beds between them and the glass entrance lobby were empty apart from a few bushes and dormant flowers, waiting to bloom in the warmer summer months.

Dotty helped Edith out of the Mercedes, and she was about to escort her to the care home's entrance when the older lady suggested, "Let's go in the back way."

Edith's room was on the first floor, facing the car park. Dotty remembered, from her first visit and tour with Aunt Beanie, that these were the cheaper rooms.

The care home's light brown furniture was supplemented with an armchair, a dressing table, and a small antique mahogany bureau with glass-fronted shelves above.

Edith approached the bureau and Dotty followed, noting the shelves held an eclectic collection of ornaments and knick-knacks, including a small porcelain bowl decorated with roses, a blue Wedgwood trinket box with a white floral motif, and a bronze cat.

"Ethel gave me the cat for Christmas. She liked cats."

Edith opened the glass doors and took out the trinket box, which she considered, before replacing it and removing the cat.

"Poor Ethel."

They heard voices outside.

"You better go," said Edith. "They don't like strangers in here."

"Will you be all right?" asked Dotty as Edith reached the door, opened it a fraction, and peered out into the corridor.

"All clear. And I'll be fine. Thank you." As Dotty left, Edith squeezed her arm.

CHAPTER THIRTY-TWO

Dotty felt tired by the time she drove onto the broken concrete yard at Meadowbank Farm and parked Nick's Mercedes beside her little Skoda, in front of the path leading to her silver-grey front door.

She climbed out and stretched as she heard Norman shout, "Hello, can I help you?"

"It's OK. It's only me," she called back as Norman approached.

"Dotty, I didn't recognise the car."

"It's Nick's. Sergeant Unwin."

He narrowed his eyes at her but didn't make any further comments apart from, "Come inside. You look as if you need a cup of tea."

As she entered the kitchen, she smelt the warm fresh smell of baking, and her stomach fluttered.

Approaching the blue Aga to heat up the kettle, she noticed fresh fruit scones arranged haphazardly on a wire rack.

Norman stood beside her and said, "Beanie's scones have turned out well. She was afraid they wouldn't rise. Tea and warm scones. Perfect. I'll see if we have some jam and I kept aside some cream from Buttercup's milking which I'll whisk up while you make the tea."

Aunt Beanie appeared. Her scarf was coming loose, with strands of white hair escaping from under it.

"I wish Norman had never suggested finding china plates for the scones. Once I started looking, I ended up down a rabbit hole. I've piles of side plates, cups and saucers, and serving dishes all over the dining room floor."

She smoothed down her hair and, as she re-tied the chocolate-brown scarf with a bow on top of her head, continued, "I thought it would be easy, as I'd already sorted stuff for your cafe at the antiques centre at Christmas time, but I was wrong."

Dotty removed the boiling kettle from the hot plate and poured water into a white enamel tea pot with a black and white cow painted on the side.

"And there's such a mismatch," moaned Aunt Beanie. "I have the service we were given when we married, and my Granny and Aunt both gave me what was left of theirs, but there must also be several generations of Devereaux crockery I can't ever remember using."

"Why don't you sell some of it at the charity tabletop sale Keya's organising at Windrush Hall?" suggested Dotty.

"Just what I was thinking," agreed Norman, as he started whisking cream with a fork.

"That will take ages. Use the electric whisk," instructed Aunt Beanie.

"It gets too thick, too quickly," Norman replied, stubbornly.

"Well, at least use the hand whisk."

Aunt Beanie placed scones on a side plate and carried them to the pine table.

Dotty sorted out teacups, teaspoons, and milk while Norman finished whipping the cream. He'd already placed a jar of raspberry jam on the table.

As Dotty poured the tea, Norman sat down and sighed, "Perfect."

"How was the fair?" asked Aunt Beanie as she took the cup Dotty offered her.

"If she even went," chuckled Norman. "She arrived back in a very sporty Mercedes."

"Really?" Aunt Beanie raised her eyebrows.

Dotty sipped her tea while Norman and Beanie watched her expectantly.

"Nick and Keya have been detained at the antique fair with a police matter, and Nick asked me to drive an elderly witness home. I expect he'll be here soon to collect his car."

"What happened at the fair? You didn't find a dead body in an oak blanket chest, did you?" grinned Aunt Beanie.

"No, she was slumped half on and half off a sofa."

Aunt Beanie gulped.

Norman stopped spreading jam on his scone and asked, "Who was?"

"An old lady called Ethel."

"The other half of Edith?" asked Aunt Beanie.

"Do you know them?" Dotty sipped her tea, gratefully.

Aunt Beanie placed her elbows on the table, and holding her cup close to her mouth, she disclosed, "They used to visit the auction house, but David caught them bidding up a painting for someone and George banned them. Shame, they were a colourful couple."

"I suppose she died of a heart attack," muttered Norman. "But it must have been a shock. Did you find her?"

Dotty nodded. "But it wasn't a heart attack. Someone strangled her, with her own scarf."

Aunt Beanie gasped and her left hand reached up to touch the bow on her head.

"Another murder. These fairs are dangerous places to visit," remarked Norman. He bit into his scone, and for a moment, concern was replaced by pleasure.

"Hiya," called Keya as she knocked on the kitchen door and entered. "Oh! Something smells nice. Freshly baked scones."

"Help yourself," said Aunt Beanie.

"I'm with Nick and PC Jenkins." Keya's face fell as she eyed the scones.

"Why don't you invite them in as well? There's plenty for everyone."

"I was hoping they'd last us all week," grumbled Norman.

Aunt Beanie glowered at him, and he smiled back sweetly.

"Good job I brought enough plates through," commented Aunt Beanie.

"I'll see to drinks," offered Dotty, standing.

Keya handed PC Jenkins a scone on a floral side plate, but he stood around, uncertain what to do.

"Sit down, Ryan," ordered Aunt Beanie. "We're all friends here." He placed his hat on the worktop and sat down next to Norman, who passed him the raspberry jam and cream.

"This is very kind of you, Mrs Devereux," said Nick politely. "I didn't realise how hungry I was."

"I'm starving," admitted Keya. "But then none of us had lunch. How was Edith, Dotty?"

"Sad. At the loss of her friend, but also her way of life. Can you believe it? She lives in the same nursing home as Uncle Cliff, at Burford?"

"No way!" exclaimed Keya.

"How does she get out to fairs?" asked Aunt Beanie. "The staff always seem very strict."

"There are ways to sneak in and out, like I did." Dotty hung her head sheepishly. "But she said Ethel used to pretend to be her younger sister. And Ethel did all the driving."

"I wonder what car she drove," pondered Nick. "I hadn't thought to look for one. Can you follow that up with Worcestershire Police, PC Jenkins, Ryan?"

Ryan removed a notebook and wrote on a page.

"So whose case is this?" asked Aunt Beanie, before biting into her scone, which was ladened with raspberry jam and whipped cream.

Nick leaned back. "Worcestershire's at the moment, unless we can find evidence to link it to Roger Dewhirst's murder."

"But Worcestershire doesn't seem that bothered about the death of an old lady," declared Keya. "They presume she died of a heart attack, despite our evidence of finding her scarf wrapped around her face and marks on her neck. They say she probably caught it on something before collapsing on the sofa. Though I've no idea what."

"Her scarf wrapped around her face?" queried Aunt Beanie.

Dotty pushed the half-eaten scone away from her. She no longer felt hungry. "It was around her mouth."

"Like a warning to someone to keep quiet," suggested Aunt Beanie.

"I suppose so," considered Keya.

"That was my conclusion," agreed Nick.

"What trouble was this old lady likely to cause?" asked Norman.

Aunt Beanie sat taller and explained, "As I explained earlier, George banned the two of them from Akemans after bidding up a painting."

"They don't actually bid or buy anything at fairs, but they often push a hesitant buyer to make a purchase," explained Dotty.

"Sounds pretty harmless to me," acknowledged Norman. "Not a reason to kill one of them."

"But we think Ethel was tied up in something else," countered Keya. "We just don't know what."

"And I'm not sure Worcestershire Police are interested in finding out," admitted Nick. "Keya and I will speak to Chief Inspector Ringrose about the case on Monday. He may want to follow up the antiques angle."

Ryan was eyeing up Dotty's unfinished scone.

She slid it in his direction, and he smiled gratefully at her and spooned raspberry jam onto the untouched half.

"And we need to speak to him about the oriental robe," spluttered Keya through a mouthful of scone.

Dotty narrowed her eyes and asked, "What robe?"

"I finished interviewing customers at the stall, the one which occupied part of the room where the body was found, and as I began questioning the stallholder, she suddenly cried out and pointed to an empty spot on the partition wall. Apparently, a silk robe, an expensive one, had been hanging there, and it had vanished. She assured me she hadn't sold it."

Dotty felt a heaviness in her stomach. "It was a chapan, from the Middle East, and it was beautiful. Purple silk with gold and silver thread brocade."

Aunt Beanie caught her eye and remarked, "Another artefact returning to a certain Middle Eastern museum?"

Dotty pursed her lips and nodded.

"I hope there isn't a pattern developing!" exclaimed Keya. "A dead body and a stolen antique at the last two fairs. And it would be a disaster if I organised another event at Windrush Hall where someone died. The charity triathlon and Christmas ball were quite enough."

Aunt Beanie turned to her and said reassuringly, "I'm sure they won't. And Norman and Dotty are trying to persuade me to take a table at your sale and sell some of my china crockery."

"Fantastic," enthused Keya. "I'll put you down for a table."

"Better make it two," mumbled Norman.

"When is it?" asked Aunt Beanie, ignoring Norman.

"The last Saturday in February, so only four weeks away." Keya's face paled. "Gosh, I've loads to do."

"I can help," offered Dotty.

"Thanks." Keya smiled appreciatively.

"And are you coming for Sunday lunch tomorrow?" asked Dotty.

Keya looked at Nick and Ryan. "We all have to work, don't we?"

"Then why don't you all come over for an early supper when you're finished?" suggested Aunt Beanie.

Dotty glanced across at Aunt Beanie. Was she just being polite, or did she also want updating on the cases?

Nick hesitated, but Ryan looked bright-eyed and keen.

Nick nodded and said, "Thank you, Mrs Devereaux. We'd be delighted."

CHAPTER THIRTY-THREE

On Sunday morning, Dotty wandered bleary-eyed into the kitchen at Meadowbank Farm.

Aunt Beanie was already sipping tea at the kitchen table. As Dotty entered, she asked, "How about accompanying me to visit Cliff this morning?"

"Aren't you going to church?"

"They're holding a short service in the care home, which I'll attend, and I thought you might like to speak to some of the residents, and check on one in particular."

"Yes, I would like to make sure Edith is OK."

Dotty parked her green Skoda in the same place she'd parked Nick's Mercedes the previous day. The weather was miserable, and she pulled the hood of her coat over her head as she climbed out of the car.

Aunt Beanie marched towards the glass-fronted entrance holding the top of her coat over her head, presumably not wanting to flatten the large pink bow of the headscarf she wore. Dotty locked her car and ran across the garden to catch up.

There were a few visitors mingling with the many residents in the central open-plan area of the care home.

A voice called, "Everyone, please find your seats. The service will begin in five minutes."

Dotty felt a tug on her coat sleeve, and she turned to the see the pale face of Edith. There were large bags under her eyes and she didn't look as if she'd slept much the previous night.

"Come with me," Edith whispered.

They sneaked out of the central area without being seen. The care home's staff were busy helping the residents into their chairs, which were arranged in rows, facing a temporary altar covered with a white cloth, with a wooden cross on top.

"I'm so glad you've come. I didn't sleep a wink last night. There's something I need to show you." Edith led Dotty to her first-floor room, where the rain drummed against her window.

"You came with Cliff's wife," remarked Edith. "I like him. He keeps himself to himself, but sometimes he likes to talk about the old days. He was a farmer and has lived in the Cotswolds all his life and has lots of interesting stories to tell."

"I'm glad he has someone to talk to. I know Aunt Beanie worries about him."

"You're his niece?"

"No, it's a nickname I picked up from his real niece, Gilly. Does she visit?"

"There were two ladies last week. One with long blonde hair and the other with bright orange curls. But they didn't stay long. Cliff wasn't in a talkative mood, and he didn't recognise either of them. I think the blonde lady was rather upset."

"That would be George, and Gilly has the orange curls. I'm glad they visited, but it must be so hard when someone you've known all your life no longer knows who you are."

Edith looked out of her window at the grey sky and murmured, "At least Ethel was saved that. She was still so full of life." Edith sniffed, turned back to Dotty, and asked, "Will the police want to interview me again?"

"I'm not sure. Worcestershire Police are in charge of Ethel's case now."

"And Roger Dewhirst's?"

"That's still with Gloucestershire Police. Nobody knows if the two are linked."

"Ethel and I were interviewed about Roger's death by that attractive policeman you were at the fair with on Saturday. But Ethel did most of the talking."

Edith wandered across to the glass-fronted case on top of her bureau. "I didn't like to bother him, or poke my nose into other people's business, but if it might help Ethel ..."

She removed the blue Wedgwood trinket box from a shelf and walked slowly across to a chipped mahogany coffee table where she emptied out its contents.

There were several brooches, one like the kingfisher Dotty had seen at the Malvern Fair, and another sparkled like diamonds and was star-shaped. There were several gold rings and a length of coloured beads.

Edith picked up a small gold and diamanté star hanging from a curved gold rod with a tiny ball on the end. It looked vaguely familiar.

Edith stared at it, apparently mesmerised by the reflected light, as she said, "I saw Keely arguing with Roger after Roger's wife made a scene at the Cotswold Antique Fair. They were in the corridor leading to the toilets, and I daren't pass them. Keely slapped Roger and turned to leave, but he grabbed her and they struggled. I think that's when she must have dropped this."

Edith held out the twinkling star and placed it in Dotty's open hand.

Of course. It was Keely's belly-button ring.

"Keely ran past me, into the toilets. Roger wanted to follow her but thought better of it and returned to the hotel. I asked Keely if she was all right, as she was holding tissues to her tummy and they turned red with blood. She sobbed and said she'd be fine, so I left to find Ethel. But you might want to give that to the sergeant."

Dotty closed her hand over the jewelled star. "Thank you, Edith. I'm sure he'll be very appreciative of this, and your information."

"I just keep thinking about Ethel, and that I should have done something to protect her."

Dotty placed her hand on Edith's arm and consoled her. "It's not your fault. There's nothing you could have done."

CHAPTER THIRTY-FOUR

Dotty spent Sunday afternoon preparing supper. She was cooking roast beef for everyone except Keya, for whom she was filling and roasting a butternut squash. She doubted Keya would eat it all, but everyone else could try a piece.

She was just sprinkling the topping over her apple and blackberry crumble when the door opened and Keya, Nick and Ryan, walked in. She wasn't used to seeing Ryan in plain clothes.

He wore a pair of jeans with a red and white stripped rugby top, with an emblem of a lion and Gloucester Rugby printed above it.

Aunt Beanie followed them and approached the sink. As she washed her hands, she announced, "I've had a very successful day clearing out the dining room and I've loads of crockery, cutlery and linen to sell at your tabletop sale, Keya. In fact, as Norman has said, only half-joking, I suspect I'll probably need two tables."

Keya's tired face brightened, and she asked, "Can I have a look?"

Aunt Beanie led her out of the kitchen, passing Norman, who walked in and asked, "Anyone for a beer?"

"I'm driving," replied Ryan, glancing at his watch. "But one now should be OK."

"We brought this." Ryan handed Norman a bottle of expensive looking red wine.

"Wonderful. I'll open it to let it breathe, and then we can have it with our roast beef."

Ryan smiled and licked his lips.

"And for the cook." Nick held out a pink cyclamen in a white pot.

"It's lovely," she replied. "Thank you."

Nick placed the pot on the worktop and took the beer Norman offered him.

Dotty washed her hands and said, "And I have something for you."

Nick raised an eyebrow.

She picked up a small plastic bag, containing the gold and diamante star Edith had given her, from the worktop and explained, "Aunt Beanie and I visited Burford Nursing Home this morning and I saw Edith. She looked very pale and is clearly missing her friend. But she took me to her room and gave me that. It's Keely's belly-button ring."

Frowning, Nick held up the plastic bag.

"How did she get hold of it?"

"She told me she saw Keely and Roger arguing after Natalie confronted Keely, and they had a tussle, which is when she thinks that was ripped off. She found Keely in the ladies, dabbing her bleeding tummy."

"Thank you, although I'm not sure it brings us any closer to finding Roger's killer. Keely's story is that she spent the time between the initial altercation and Roger's death in the toilets, and she might be telling the truth, although she did forget to mention her argument with Roger. I wonder."

"Oh, wow!" exclaimed Keya as she rushed into the kitchen, followed by Aunt Beanie. "I've just agreed to buy most of Aunt Beanie's crockery and some of her cutlery and linen. It'll be perfect for my cafe."

"What cafe?" asked Nick.

Keya scratched her neck and looked sheepish. "I'm not sure yet, but when I'm ready to open one, I'll have fantastic cups, saucers and side plates."

"Does that mean you won't be taking a table at the fair?" asked Dotty. She poured boiling water into a pan of sliced runner beans.

"There's plenty more where those came from," confirmed Norman.

Aunt Beanie narrowed her eyes and then shrugged her shoulders. "You're right, of course. And it did feel very cathartic clearing out drawers and cupboards today, although it's also rather sad."

Dotty removed the joint of beef from the top oven and placed it on a glass heatproof mat. "We'll let it sit while I make the gravy and then will you carve Norman?"

"I'll be happy to." He opened a drawer and rummaged around until he found a large knife and a long carving fork.

Eyeing it, Nick said, "And we've got plenty of news for you."

"Then let's sit down at the table and you can tell us," instructed Aunt Beanie.

Norman and Dotty remained standing as the others took their seats, with Aunt Beanie at the head of the table.

Nick sat down next to her and looked across at Ryan, who was seated beside Keya. "Why don't you start since you extracted and ran Billy Edmunds' fingerprints from the can of Coke he drank at the fair?"

With her back to the table, as she stirred the gravy on the cooler Aga hot plate, adding juice from the resting beef, Dotty heard Ryan clear his throat and begin, "Billy has an extensive record, mostly for theft. He started with shoplifting and moved on to cars. He was arrested for fighting outside a pub but released with a caution."

Nick added, "Those in the antique fair world seemed to know and tolerate Billy, and he hasn't been arrested for over two years. There's nothing from his record, or witness statements, to suggest that he's escalated to murder."

"But he had fallen out with Roger over that vase," raised Dotty, turning towards the table.

"But Roger was the one annoyed with him," responded Keya. "Billy made him look like a fool and made a profit from him."

"And I think Billy would have taken the direct approach and punched Roger, or hit him with one of the glass pieces on the stall," added Nick. "He probably has a temper, but it would die down quickly. I can't see him removing a weapon from another stall and returning to kill Roger."

Dotty removed the cloths and tin foil covering the beef and nodded to Norman, who approached with his carving knife and fork.

She asked. "So you're ruling out Billy?"

"Yes, unless we find any new evidence to implicate him," confirmed Nick.

"And he can't have had anything to do with Ethel's death as he was downstairs with you when she was killed," added Keya.

"But he could have stolen the chapan robe," murmured Dotty.

CHAPTER THIRTY-FIVE

Norman carved while the others filled their plates with the contents of the bowls and dishes Dotty placed on heatproof mats on the worktop.

"Roast beef, roast potatoes and Yorkshire puddings," announced Ryan happily. "I haven't had these since I left home."

"When was that?" asked Aunt Beanie.

"Six months ago," replied Ryan, placing a second Yorkshire pudding on his already crammed plate. "My mum's boyfriend moved in and made my life hell. I don't think he liked having a policeman living in the same house."

Keya cut into one half of the roasted butternut squash. "This smells dreamy. Have you used thyme?"

"Yes, we've kept a plant growing on the windowsill," confirmed Dotty.

"Why not go on a cookery course, Ryan?" suggested Keya. "Olivia Hambleton runs some starter courses."

"I went to visit her again today," volunteered Nick as he sat down. "Her husband works in London during the week, and they seem to have a very comfortable lifestyle. Although she was obviously annoyed about Roger Dewhirst's bounced cheque, I don't think £2,000 is that much of a deal to her."

"I agree," confirmed Keya, as she took her seat. "I've been looking into her and her husband financially, and I can't see any irregularities. No large bills left unpaid or gambling debts."

"So while we can't rule Olivia out, we are putting her to one side for the moment," reasoned Nick.

Dotty was the last to sit down, and she took the space next to Nick, opposite Ryan. The apple and blackberry crumble was keeping warm in the bottom oven, and she only needed to reheat the custard before she served it. She felt weary but content as she watched everyone tuck into their food.

Nick put his knife and fork down and turned to her. "Your friend Quinn Hughes is a far more interesting character."

"Really?"

"Ryan, tell us what you've discovered," suggested Nick.

Ryan turned pink as he finished chewing while everyone watched him.

Gulping, he said, "Quinn Hughes has been associated with several failed business ventures. The last one cost him £30,000."

Norman whistled. He poured himself a glass of red wine and passed the bottle across the table. Dotty poured herself half a glass and passed it on to Nick.

Nick picked up the bottle and said, "I suspect the reason Quinn has been pushing his parents to recover the money they gave Roger is so he can have it for his new business venture. And his parents are exactly who they claim to be. Ryan checked them too."

"What business is he proposing now?" asked Aunt Beanie.

"Something to do with recycling," Ryan replied.

"Do you think he killed Roger over the money?" asked Dotty.

"If he did, it was pretty stupid as it didn't help him recover it, but I'm not ruling him out," asserted Nick. "He's rented out his flat in Reading and moved back in with his parents, but Ryan didn't find any creditors, and the money he lost was his own, from re-mortgaging his flat."

"You've done a lot of work," Aunt Beanie observed, "but I'm not sure it's moved your investigation forward."

Nick nodded. "True, but maybe we'll get somewhere with Dotty's lead."

"What's that?" asked Keya, her eyes shining.

"She discovered where the blood came from on the paper towels you found in the ladies," replied Nick.

"Where?" asked Keya.

"From Keely." Dotty explained, "She and Roger had a tussle, and her belly-button ring was ripped off. I spoke to Edith again this morning at the care home. She witnessed it."

"Ow! That must have hurt. But I doubt it was a reason for killing Roger," conceded Keya.

Nick said, "No, but she did have a strong motive to kill him. He'd told her his wife was disabled, and he was tied to her as her carer. Which was complete rubbish. And apart from Edith's statement, nobody else saw Keely before Roger's death. Ryan, we need to visit her tomorrow. We can go first thing in the morning, before we visit Ethel's house in Gloucester."

"I thought Worcestershire Police were investigating Ethel's death," said Dotty.

"They are, but as her house is in our jurisdiction, they're more than happy for us to follow up and visit it," explained Nick.

Keya stabbed a piece of butternut squash and asked, "Where in Gloucester is it?"

Ryan removed his notebook and read out, "Number five, Jasmine Street."

Keya winced. "There's nothing sweet smelling about that road. The council has been trying to evict the few remaining residents. It's pretty grim and many of the houses are boarded-up or their windows are broken and their front doors graffitied. It's zoned for redevelopment."

Nick smiled at Ryan and said, "You better bring your hard hat, Constable, and we'll take the squad car."

"Miss Clarke might not like that," countered Ryan.

"No," mused Nick.

Saturday's antique fair flashed into Dotty's mind. "I've just remembered. I'm sure I saw Keely yesterday."

"Really?" asked Nick in surprise.

"Yes, she ducked behind a marble pillar in the front hall when I was leaving with Edith, but I'm sure it was her. And the stall next to the pillar was selling glass and porcelain, like the items Roger sold."

Keya mused, "I wonder if she had her own side business or if Roger stored some stock with her."

Nick lifted his wineglass. "Something else for us to ask about tomorrow, Ryan."

CHAPTER THIRTY-SIX

On Monday, Dotty returned to Akemans and spent her day sorting through items from the previous week's auction.

Several customers arrived to collect their purchases and a delivery van took away a wardrobe and dining room table and chairs.

She and Norman were standing in the auction room surveying what was left when George appeared and said, "Most of this can go forward to February or March's sale. But let's ask the owner to collect these lamps, and Dotty, you can take what's left on the tables in the small room for your stall. All the silverware went, which is excellent. And none of the owners of the remaining pictures want them back."

Norman turned to Dotty and remarked, "I better get on. I spend my time moving furniture from here to the store and back again. Is this all my life is worth?"

Dotty smiled at him. "But you have Buttercup, and the farm, and you're not working full time. I thought you'd enjoyed your walking. What else do you want to do in your spare time?"

Norman frowned, "I'm not sure, but I'm not getting any younger."

Dotty wandered through to the smaller room at the end of the auction house.

She was pleased that the glasses she'd unwrapped and arranged on a table had sold, as had all the silverware and jewellery from the glass-fronted cases.

Quite a few pictures remained on the walls. She removed a collection of four small ones. Each depicted a fruit, whole on the branch and then cut in half. They would suit a kitchen wall and she had space on her stall to display them.

The previous summer, Dotty had started a bargain stall on the first floor of the antique centre, and she often received unwanted items from other stallholders in the centre and from auctions. She sold the items for a few pounds, and the stall had proved popular.

The rest of the pictures would be packed away, either for future sales, if there was space, or to be disposed of. That was the part Dotty hated most. Someone's treasured possessions ending up in a rubbish dump.

Dotty was wrapping pottery animal figurines when she heard Keya call, "Hiya."

Keya walked into the small room wearing her black and white police uniform, followed by Ryan, who was also in uniform.

"This feels like an official visit," remarked Dotty.

"It is. We've come to formally interview you about the missing Oriental robe, as you appear to be the last person to see it."

"Middle Eastern. It wasn't Chinese."

"Whatever. But first, you've got to hear about Ryan and Nick's visit to Ethel's house."

Ryan looked down at the floor and shuffled his feet.

Dotty placed the wrapped figurine of a rabbit in a cardboard box and suggested, "I'll make us all a cup of tea and we can share one of Aunt Beanie's scones which I brought with me today."

Keya sat down on the grey sofa in reception and Ryan folded himself into a grey tub chair. They both put their hats down on the reclaimed-elm coffee table. Dotty also placed a white plate on the table with two halves of a scone, spread with raspberry jam.

As she returned to the kitchen to make tea and coffee, she heard Keya say, "Tuck in, Ryan."

"Coffee, perfect," acknowledged Keya, taking a cup from Dotty. "I need to keep my wits about me today."

Ryan had also asked for coffee and Dotty settled herself on the sofa next to Keya with a cup of tea. Ryan eyed the remaining half of the scone.

Keya looked longing at it and then pushed the plate toward Ryan. "Go on, you need it more than me, and then you can tell us about Ethel's house."

Ryan looked content as he wiped crumbs from his mouth with the back of his hand. "If tea and cakes are your interrogation technique to encourage people to talk, it works." He grinned. "So you won't believe what we found at Ethel's house."

"What?" asked Dotty, playing along.

"Cats. At least twenty of them," announced Ryan. "They had some sort of automatic food and water dispensers, but the smell." He grimaced. "And cat hairs covered the threadbare sofa and armchair, as well as the worn carpet."

"Edith told me Ethel liked cats. She showed me a small bronze cat ornament Ethel gave her," said Dotty.

"What's going to happen to the cats?" asked Keya.

"I called the RSPCA," Ryan replied. "It's not as if I could ask any neighbours to look after them. The only other occupant on the street was a man in his eighties and the council told me they moved him to a care home last week."

Dotty sat back and said, "So Ethel would have been the only person still living on the street. The only one standing in the way of the redevelopment I presume. Do you know how far along that is?"

Ryan nodded. "The local council have bought up the remaining houses and agreed to sell them, and the adjoining empty street, to a developer who wants to build executive apartments. A planning application has already been submitted."

Keya's eyes widened in understanding and she exclaimed, "Do you think someone bumped Ethel off because she wouldn't leave her house and was preventing the redevelopment?"

"Nick, Sergeant Unwin, thinks that's a distinct possibility. But what he can't work out is how someone would know she was at the antique fair. It would have been far easier to visit her at home and make her death look like an accident. And with the street being empty, it could have been days, even weeks, before anyone found her."

"The cats would make a noise," considered Dotty, "but I can see where Nick's coming from. So, what are you going to do next?"

"We passed our findings on about the land and redevelopment to Worcestershire Police," Ryan said.

Keya shrugged. "So we'll have to wait and see what progress they make. But now we need to take your statement about the chapan robe, and then I have to attend a village meeting at Lemington."

Dotty grinned. "What are they complaining about now?"

Keya rolled her eyes. "It's still the new owner of the hall."

Ryan cleared his throat and asked, "When did you first see the chapan robe?"

Dotty thought back and began, "I was with Keya and we were looking round the stalls at the fair. Keya wanted to speak to the stallholders about the stolen copper jug."

Keya nodded. "That's right. I left you outside the library and went to speak to stallholders in the main gallery."

Dotty gasped. "And that's when I thought I saw David Rook entering a room off the main corridor. I followed him, but couldn't see him anywhere in the room. That's when I noticed the robe hanging up on the partition wall of the stall and it was beautiful.

"The stallholder was speaking to a customer, and I was going to wait to speak to her about David, but Nick called me from the doorway. That's the only time I saw the robe. I was busy with Nick interviewing Billy, and then we were all trying to find Ethel." Dotty broke off, thinking of poor Ethel.

"Thank you," said Ryan.

"Please don't be sad," said Keya. "Hey, why don't you come along to my meeting? It might be entertaining."

Dotty tucked a strand of hair behind her ear. "I'm not sure."

"Well, at least give me a lift there so Ryan can return to the station. And we can discuss plans for the charity tabletop sale on the way. Ryan's given me details of a local firm who can provide tables and chairs, and they give discounts for charity events."

"Has Jay chosen a charity?" asked Dotty.

"He wants to split the proceeds between the oldest and youngest in our community. So he's considering a couple of children's charities and some which support the elderly. Apparently Burford Care Home is raising funds for a new minibus after the gearbox went in their old one. They want to be able to take their residents out on trips."

"Edith would like that," considered Dotty, "but I'm not sure about Uncle Cliff."

Ryan cleared his throat. "If you're OK giving Keya a lift, I'll return to the station."

Keya gave Dotty a pleading look.

"Ok, I'll drop you there," Dotty conceded. "But you'll need to arrange someone to collect you. I don't think I can bear sitting through a long meeting with people moaning and complaining."

Ryan picked up his hat.

"Before you go, any news on Keely?" asked Dotty.

"She wasn't very forthcoming, but when we told her a witness had seen her at the fair on Saturday, she finally admitted she'd been there. Roger had stored some stock with her, some of the better quality items actually, and as he'd already paid for the stall, she thought she might as well go. She hired a van for the weekend and slept in it on Saturday night."

Dotty tapped her fingers on the table. "And her alibi for Roger's death?"

Ryan replied, "She insists she stayed in the ladies' toilets until just before Roger's body was found."

"But she was also at the fair on Saturday, when Ethel was killed," considered Dotty.

"Oh, do you think there's a link? That Keely killed Roger and Ethel?" asked Keya.

"I don't know," admitted Dotty. "But there could be. Someone wanted to silence Ethel. Perhaps she saw whoever killed Roger."

CHAPTER THIRTY-SEVEN

Dotty drove Keya to Lemington as the darkness gathered around them. Her headlights picked up a single-storey, white, prefabricated corrugated iron building, with a light in an enclosed plastic case positioned above the entrance door.

As she parked, Keya peered out of the windscreen and muttered, "If only the villagers would act nicely and welcome the new lord of the manor, instead of protesting against him, they might receive a sizeable donation towards a new village hall. One with heating and a proper kitchen, and enough space for the toddler group and keep fit."

"What time is your meeting?" asked Dotty.

Keya checked her watch. "In fifteen minutes, but let's go inside, in case people arrive early."

They entered the village hall and Keya gasped. "I wasn't expecting this."

Four serving staff, wearing black, were busy placing sandwiches on platters and cakes on pretty floral stands on tables arranged along one wall of the hall. Another figure was arranging bottles and glasses on a separate table.

She turned to Dotty, smiling, and said, "Aren't you pleased you came now? You won't have to worry about cooking supper tonight."

"Sergeant Varma," a smooth, well-spoken male voice said, with a hint of a foreign accent.

They turned and this time, Dotty inhaled in surprise. The man approaching them was Tariq, one of the Arab men she'd met with David at Bath Showground's antique fair.

Tariq shook hands with Keya as he apologised. "My father sends his regards, but he's been called away to a business meeting. So he asked me to represent him and, as a welcome gift to the villagers, he's provided what we hope is some traditional British food."

Dotty turned and watched one of the serving staff removing scotch eggs from a container, which were cut in half with vibrant orange yolks. Another server was arranging individual pork pies on a plate.

"It certainly looks very impressive, Mr Kazem, and it's generous of your father. Although I doubt it will appease the villagers."

Keya and Tariq exchanged knowing smiles.

Keya continued, "And can I introduce my friend and chauffeur this evening, Dotty Sayers?"

Tariq held out his hand and as Dotty shook it, he said, "But we've met before. With David Rook."

"Yes, at the Bath Showground antique fair."

"Of course, and do you live in the village?" asked Tariq politely.

Dotty shook her head. "No, as Keya, Sergeant Varma said, I drove her here for this evening's meeting. I live about ten miles away, in Fairford."

When Tariq looked blank, she added, "A small town near Cirencester."

"Ah, Cirencester I know. Very historic, and with an excellent gentleman's outfitters."

Tariq thumbed the open front of his brown tweed jacket. Then he leaned towards Dotty and confided, "We can be outsiders together. The local people don't approve of my father buying the hall, even though it's been empty for several years and needs a considerable amount of renovation work."

The door opened and an elderly couple entered. Keya moved across to help them.

"And will you make this your permanent home?" asked Dotty.

Tariq inclined his head to one side, and replied, "When we're in the

UK, and I hope to spend more time here, but alas, I have to travel to Istanbul this week." His eyes suddenly widened. "But you must come with us."

"Me?" Dotty gasped.

"Yes, David is joining us to visit one of the world's largest antique fairs, and with all those Ottoman treasures on display, it's quite spectacular."

"I don't think so." Dotty shook her head. "It sounds rather expensive and, besides, David prefers to go on his trips alone."

"Nonsense," countered Tariq. "In fact, David has already asked my father about bringing you along. He said it would be a great experience. There's space in my father's jet and he's hired out the top floor of the Four Seasons Hotel, so you'll have your own room, and you don't need to worry about the cost."

"Well ..."

"That's settled," declared Tariq.

Dotty smiled, a flutter in the bottom of her stomach. "I'll have to speak to David and ask for time off work."

"Yes, yes, we'll arrange it with David," agreed Tariq.

More people entered the village hall. A woman pushed past Tariq, the hood of her grey hoodie covering her head, and Dotty spotted a pink emblem on her back. A picture of a pair of scissors.

Something stirred within her mind and she felt cold.

"Are you OK?" asked Tariq. "You're very pale."

"I think I need a drink. Will you excuse me?"

Dotty left Tariq as she heard a male voice boom, "Mr Kazem, where is your father tonight? Too busy to join us, is he?"

She followed the grey hooded figure to the drinks table.

The wearer pushed back the hood to reveal her sleek bob of dark hair and she said, "Two gin and tonics. Make them doubles."

Another server approached Dotty.

"Just a tonic water, please," she requested. "I'm driving."

The other woman turned to her and said, "You're not from the village."

"No," agreed Dotty, trying to keep the conversation on a civil note. "I drove my friend, Sergeant Varma, here." Dotty noted the scissor logo on the front of the hoodie and the words 'A Cut Above'.

"I suppose that's all right then." The woman picked up two full glasses and turned to leave.

"A Cut Above is a salon in Cirencester, isn't it?" asked Dotty.

The woman turned back and confirmed, "Yes. On Silver Street. I work there as a beautician. Only part time. We don't need the money, but it gets me out of the house and Natalie's a good boss."

"Is that Natalie Wright?"

"Sure. Do you know her?"

"I've met her and seen her around. Do you happen to know what car she drives?"

The woman regarded her suspiciously. "Not that it's any of your business, but one of those large 4x4s. Black, I think." The woman turned and left.

Dotty needed to find Keya. She thought she knew how Roger had been killed.

CHAPTER THIRTY-EIGHT

Dotty turned away from the drinks table in Lemington Village Hall and looked across at Tariq to see a crowd had formed around him.

The volume of voices in the room was increasing as people tried to make themselves heard and she saw a few people gesticulating at Tariq. One man was even shaking his fist.

The atmosphere in the room was changing. She could feel the angry undertones.

Suddenly, a sandwich arced through the air and landed with a plop on a man's bald head. It might have been funny if the second missile, a vol-au-vent, hadn't found its mark and hit Tariq on the cheek.

Calmly, he wiped the grey sludge - the vol-au-vent must have contained a mushroom filling - off his face with a red spotted handkerchief.

Dotty heard Keya call for order, but the villagers weren't in a mood to listen. Keya jammed her flat police hat firmly on her head as more edible projectiles rained down. A cupcake landed on top of her hat and bounced off, leaving a yellow smudge of icing.

Keya glanced across at her and they locked eyes for several seconds before Keya turned and whispered something to Tariq, who she was now standing next to as she tried to ward off jostling villagers.

Tariq and Keya pushed through the jeering crowd towards Dotty and without losing momentum, Tariq caught Dotty's arm and Keya bundled them both out of the rear fire escape door before she returned to the fray.

"I'm pleased my father isn't here," remarked Tariq calmly as he wiped the remains of food from his tweed jacket with his handkerchief.

"I'm sorry. I don't know why they are so anti you and your family," apologised Dotty. She knew she shouldn't, but she felt a sense of responsibility for the villagers' appalling behaviour.

"Sergeant Varma says it's because they have a common enemy. They spend so much time fighting each other that they need to take a break, and direct their anger and frustration at our family, as newcomers to the village."

"Well, I think they should grow up," Dotty declared. "And I'd like to go home, but I can't leave Keya in there, on her own."

"She told me she'd called for backup, so hopefully we won't have to wait too long. Let me walk you to your car," offered Tariq.

Slowly, they made their way around the village hall and back to the entrance and car park where Dotty's Skoda was parked on its own. The villagers must all have walked.

They heard a siren in the distance and watched as blue and white flashing lights approached and a police car parked beside Dotty's car.

"What's this about a food fight in the village hall?" asked Chief Inspector Ringrose as he peeled himself out of the car.

Ryan appeared from the driver's side.

"Quick," called Dotty. "Keya's in there on her own."

Ryan's tall figure bounded towards the front door of the village hall and he disappeared inside.

Chief Inspector Ringrose approached Tariq and said, "My apologies for the unfriendly welcome you're receiving from the inhabitants of Lemington. My team and I are working on community relations, but clearly, we have a long way to go."

The door opened and the lady with the grey hoodie, who'd once again pulled her hood over her head, emerged and disappeared into the gloom, clutching a bottle of what Dotty fancied was gin.

Next, Ryan appeared escorting the elderly couple who had arrived at the beginning. They each clasped their wooden walking sticks in one hand, and were carrying white paper napkins in their free hands, presumably filled with food from the buffet.

Three young men stumbled out of the door holding cans of beer. One called across to his mate, "That showed him, didn't it?"

Tariq said in a resigned tone, "I don't think my father's welcome buffet was well received."

"Oh, I wouldn't say that," counted the chief inspector. "It's the most cordial I've seen the residents for some time, and it might even save Sergeant Varma several trips to resolve petty disputes over the coming weeks."

Two middle-aged women emerged from the village hall. "I'm sorry for cutting branches off your silver birch."

"That's OK," replied her companion. "They were hanging over your fence. And I'll try not to park in front of your gate again."

Chief Inspector Ringrose crossed his arms. "See what I mean."

More people emerged, but there was no sign of Keya or Ryan.

"I hope Keya's OK," Dotty muttered to herself.

Several minutes passed before Keya emerged from the village hall. She looked as if she'd been the target in a multi-coloured paint balling game, as she was covered in circles of coloured icing.

"Look at me," she moaned, "I'll have to clean my whole uniform."

"Great cakes," acknowledged Ryan as he followed Keya, a half-eaten cupcake in his hand.

Tariq stepped forward and said, "Help yourself, Constable. The left overs will only be thrown away. And I suppose I'll have to pay the catering staff extra to clean the hall tonight."

Ryan returned to the village hall.

As Keya reached Dotty, Tariq and the chief inspector, Tariq said, "I know you've tried your best with the residents, and I'm sorry for what happened this evening. It did the opposite of building bridges. But we're going away for a month, so hopefully they'll have calmed down by the time we return."

Keya muttered, "I doubt it. This lot have long memories."

Now her friend was safe, and the situation had calmed down, Dotty felt she could leave. "I should go home," she said. "Will Ryan give you a lift?"

Keya nodded.

Tariq turned to Dotty and said, "I'm sorry you've been caught up in village politics, but you will speak to David, won't you? About Istanbul."

Keya frowned and asked, "Istanbul?"

"I'll explain tomorrow," replied Dotty, lowering her voice.

Ryan appeared in the doorway of the village hall, holding a cardboard box. As he strode towards them, he said, "I collected and packaged as much as I could. Keya, yours is the green bag, which only contains vegetarian food. Sir, you and Dotty can choose either of the remaining bags and I'll take the box with whatever's left."

He turned to Tariq and said, "Mr Kazem, thanks so much for this. It'll save me cooking for a few days."

Tariq smiled. "I'm pleased someone appreciates my father's hospitality."

As Keya and Dotty both removed plastic bags from the box, Dotty whispered, "I think I know how Roger was killed."

Keya yawned. "Can it wait until tomorrow? After I've filed my report about how well this evening went."

"I suppose so," replied Dotty slowly. But she realised that just telling the police her theory wouldn't really work, so she asked, "Do you think Nick could arrange for Keely and Natalie to be at Charbury Castle Hotel? I think we all need to return to the crime scene to see how it was done."

"Do you think one of them killed Roger?" Keya blurted, suddenly more alert.

Dotty bit her lip and nodded.

"Which one?"

"I can't say, not until we've run through what happened. So, can you see if Nick will arrange the meeting?"

CHAPTER THIRTY-NINE

Dotty was still sorting through items in the smaller auction room on Tuesday morning when Keya rang her.

"A meeting at Charbury Castle Hotel has been arranged for this afternoon," she said.

"Despite Natalie Wright's protests, we're meeting at two-thirty so that we can go outside if necessary, while it's still light. I just hope Keely Clarke turns up. She was complaining about having to come, so we've sent Ryan to pick her up."

"Great. I'll see you later." Dotty felt slightly nauseous. Last night she'd had a flash of inspiration as to how Roger's murder was committed, and by whom. But today, in the auction house, she was less certain.

"Dorothy, here you are," declared David Rook. "I've been looking for you. I've just come off the phone with Tariq Kazem who was telling me all about a colourful encounter you both had with some locals last night."

"I'm glad he saw the funny side of it. The villagers behaved terribly and were very rude, considering the food and drink Tariq's father laid on for them."

David nodded, "I don't think Ahmad would have been so understanding. Tariq said it was a blessing his father had been called away. But I believe he spoke to you about our upcoming trip to Istanbul. I had suggested you join us. It would be a fabulous experience. A real hands-on education."

"And you don't mind me tagging along?"

David narrowed his eyes. "Why should I mind?"

"I just …" but Dotty didn't finish her sentence. She had no idea what David normally did on his trips, but if he was willing to include her in this one, she wasn't going to turn the opportunity down.

"We're leaving on Friday. You'll need some smart outfits, dresses and that, but nothing too revealing." He paused before adding, "Marion knows the kind of thing. I'll get her to speak to you and the pair of you can go shopping if need be. I'll add the cost to Ahmad's bill."

"But what about George, and my work here?" asked Dotty.

"Don't worry about that," David replied dismissively. "I'll speak to George, and Marion will cover for you here. It'll stop her getting bored at home while I'm away and it's too cold to play golf."

David turned and left Dotty to finish packing the unsold paintings into a box. Norman would move them to the storeroom when he was next in.

Dotty arrived at Charbury Castle Hotel just after two o'clock. It had been a glorious drive, and she'd taken the smaller country roads rather than the main A417.

She knew it was still winter, and the temperature was only single figures, but the sky was a pleasant grey-blue with wispy clouds floating slowly across it.

She passed a wood and was delighted to see the heads of snowdrops hanging like white bells, proclaiming the start of spring.

A police patrol car was already parked in one of the visitor spaces in front of the hotel and she pulled up next to it. There was no sign of the occupants.

There were two marquees, though, in exactly the same place as they had been for the antique fair, at the side of the hotel, and a third was being erected by a group of workmen.

As she entered the hotel, through the revolving doors, she spotted a sign announcing the hotel was hosting a wedding fair at the weekend.

Dotty surveyed the seating area to the right of the reception where the smaller stalls selling jewellery and silverware had been located during the fair. She didn't recognise anyone sitting there.

She turned left and round a corner into the bar. Ryan was balanced on a stool, cradling a mug of tea or coffee, while Keely, sitting on a bench seat opposite him, was drinking a dark liquid from a highball glass. Coke, but Dotty wondered if it also contained a shot of vodka.

Ryan smiled slowly in relief when he saw her and stood up, offering her the stool.

"Thank you. Do you know how long Sergeants Unwin and Varma will be?" She thought she should use their professional titles given the importance of the situation, and in front of one of the suspects.

"Five minutes, ma'am," replied Ryan, equally formally.

They sat with Keely in uncomfortable silence until Ryan's radio crackled.

"Sergeant Unwin has asked us to meet him outside, at the front of the hotel."

The three of them trooped back through reception and out of the revolving door.

As they approached Sergeant Unwin, who was wearing a slick grey suit and purple tie, he said, "Thank you for joining us, Miss Clarke."

"Can't see the point," she muttered.

Keya was wearing her police uniform and, as Dotty regarded her, she admitted, "Yes, it's my spare jacket. The other is at the dry cleaners."

"So we're only waiting for Mrs Wright," Nick remarked. "I do hope I don't have to call a squad car to collect her."

They waited another minute in silence until Dotty saw a large, black 4x4 turn into the hotel's drive. "I think this might be her," she said.

As she climbed out of her car, Natalie Wright declared, "This better not take long. I've already cancelled two clients."

"That's a nice car," admired Dotty.

"Thank you," replied Natalie in a slightly irritated tone.

"I bet you could drive it almost anywhere, on all sorts of terrain."

Natalie snapped, "I stick to tarmac."

Which Dotty didn't think was entirely true. There were specks of mud around the rear light, which could have appeared after Natalie pulled off a narrow road, to allow another vehicle to pass, but it was more likely she'd driven along a field, or muddy track.

Nick cleared his throat. "Where would you like to start, Dotty?"

"In the marquee, if we're allowed. Then we can run through events as they happened at the antique fair."

Ryan escorted an unwilling Keely around the side of the hotel to the marquees, and everyone else followed silently behind them. The marquee closest to the hotel was empty inside, except for a pile of trestle tables.

Dotty felt nervous. This was her show. But what if she was wrong?

She took a deep breath and stepped forward. "Ryan, why don't you be Roger for our reconstruction? Can you put up a table and stand behind it with Keely."

Ryan carried a wooden trestle table across to the space where Keely stood as she said, "I think this is where our stall was. Roger was delighted we were near the entrance."

Ryan wrestled with the rusty metal legs of the table, but finally he grunted in satisfaction and turned it upright.

"Put it here," directed Keely, who seemed to be taking the reconstruction seriously.

Natalie, on the other hand, was scrolling through her phone, ignoring them all.

"Keya, if you and I stand in the doorway. Nick, you just observe, and Natalie, can you enter the tent as you did that Saturday?"

Natalie rolled her eyes, pocketed her phone, and strode towards the entrance where Dotty and Keya stood.

She turned on her heels and walked back towards the table.

"Were you alone?" asked Dotty.

"No, Linda and Julie were with me," sneered Natalie.

"So what happened next?" Dotty ignored Natalie's angry tone.

'I approached the stall and saw Roger, and then I saw Keely." She spat out Keely's name.

"And you were sure it was that way round?" When Dotty had entered the marquee, she'd only seen Keely standing behind the stall.

"Yes," confirmed Natalie. "I was furious, seeing her standing there with my husband."

"Really, so why did you shout, 'Where's Roger?'" asked Dotty. She had only just remembered Natalie's words from the fair.

Keely seemed to be struggling to follow the discussion, and she was frowning in concentration.

Then she asked, "How did you know who I was? You were very rude, you know. Calling me all sorts of names. What if I'd just been minding the stall while Roger nipped to the gents, or was just helping him out?"

Ryan nodded at Keely. "That's a good point."

She smiled appreciatively back at him and smoothed down her hair.

Beside Dotty, Keya laughed, but quickly coughed to cover it up.

Natalie scowled and then hissed, "But I was right, wasn't I?"

Nick cleared his throat and asked, "So what happened next?"

"Roger sneaked out of the marquee." Keely pushed the much taller Ryan towards the marquee entrance. "Natalie and I saw him and followed him out."

"Go on then," encouraged Nick to Ryan. Ryan and Keely walked out of the marquee.

"Mrs Wright?"

Natalie glared at Nick before turning and following Ryan and Keely. She shoved Keya out of the way with her shoulder as she pushed through the entrance door.

"Someone's not happy about your reconstruction, Dotty," Nick observed.

"But I think Keely's enjoying herself with Ryan." Keya giggled as they joined the others outside.

"I followed Roger into the hotel, through the side door to the bar," stated Keely, apparently happy to provide the information.

"And you, Mrs Wright?" asked Nick.

"I went home, or at least I got in my car and drove away."

Dotty wrinkled her forehead. She was sure Natalie was lying, and that she had also followed Roger into the hotel, but nobody had seen her.

Dotty suggested, "Why don't I pretend to be Natalie and go to her car, while you all go with Keely and she can explain what happened next? Can I have your car keys, please?" Dotty held out her hand.

"Why? You're not driving my car." Natalie clutched her bag to her chest.

Dotty had thought about driving it, but she shook her head and replied, "No, I won't."

Nick raised an eyebrow at Dotty.

She gave him an imploring look, and he nodded and turned to Natalie. Dotty was relieved to hear him say, "Please give me your car keys."

Reluctantly, Natalie handed them over and Nick passed them to Dotty. He asked, "Shall we meet you inside?"

"Yes, I know where you'll be."

CHAPTER FORTY

Keya, Natalie, and Nick followed Ryan and Keely into the hotel. Dotty turned towards Natalie's car, her heart pumping hard.

She was certain Natalie had killed her husband. Before they started the walk through, she hadn't been certain if it was her or Keely.

But it was Keely who'd asked the pertinent question. How had Natalie known who she was? That she was Roger's lover. As Keely pointed out herself, she could just have been helping out on the stall or covering for Roger.

No, Natalie had expected to find Keely there, and she'd gone straight to nuclear, as if wanting to make a scene.

And unlike Keely, who appeared to be enjoying the reconstruction, Natalie was decidedly uncomfortable.

But nobody knew when Natalie left the antique fair, and nobody had seen her there until she walked into The Orangery where her friends were having lunch.

Except, Dotty thought she had. But how to prove it? She walked around Natalie's car, noting more dried mud.

Then she clicked the key fob and unlocked it. She searched the front of the car but didn't find what she was looking for. She opened the rear boot and peered inside.

There was a pair of muddy boots, a rain jacket and, hidden beneath it, a grey hoodie with a pink pair of scissors printed on the back. She picked it up and turned it over. On the front was a smaller pair of pink scissors and above them was printed 'A Cut Above'.

Dotty removed the hoodie and stuffed it inside her white linen tote bag with a picture of Van Gogh's Sunflowers on the front.

She locked the car and returned to the hotel. As she expected, she found everyone standing in the corridor leading to the ladies' toilets.

Ryan looked alarmed as Keely play-acted having a fight with him and then turning, crying out and running into the ladies.

Keely came out of the toilets and Nick said, "Thank you. That was very realistic. And what did you do next?"

"I was bleeding badly, so I stayed in the ladies until it stopped. Ethel ... or was it Edith? ... saw me."

"Edith," confirmed Nick. "And we've spoken to her, and she's even given us your belly button ring."

"Oh great, can I have it back?"

"We'll see. It's evidence at the moment."

Keely's face fell. "That was about the only thing he gave me. A star-shaped belly button ring." She shrugged her shoulders.

Dotty asked, "Did Roger like stars?"

"Oh yes, they were his favourite shape," confirmed Keely enthusiastically. "He said stars represented truth and knowledge."

"And he also gave you a star-shaped piece of jewellery, didn't he, Natalie?" Dotty turned to her.

Natalie started in surprise. She looked as if she was about to deny the statement, but instead she admitted, "A star-shaped diamond brooch."

"Which you were wearing at the antique fair?"

Natalie nodded.

"And which you'll be able to show Sergeant Varma when she accompanies you home."

Keya's eyes widened.

But Natalie glanced nervously from Dotty to Keya and back. "I'm not sure where it is," she muttered.

"Really?" replied Dotty, theatrically. "When - what did you say? Giving it to you was one of the few romantic gestures your husband made? And as you were wearing it, the day he died, I'd have thought you'd treasure it. Even wear it in his memory. That is, if you still have it."

"Of course I do," Natalie bristled. "I'm just not sure where."

Nick reclaimed control of the reconstruction. "So what happened next? Miss Clarke is in the ladies and Mrs Wright is driving her car."

Keely volunteered, "When the bleeding had stopped, and I finally had the courage to leave the ladies, I returned to the marquee. Only to find Roger dead." She broke into tears and spluttered, "Poor, poor Roger."

Dotty caught Natalie give Keely a look of pure malice.

"And what about you, Mrs Wright?" Nick asked.

Natalie squared her shoulders. "I realised I couldn't let Roger's behaviour and bit-on-the-side ruin my day. Besides, I'd stranded my friends, so I turned around and drove back to the hotel. I found them eating in The Orangery, but when I arrived, they told me Roger was dead."

"How did you know where your friends were?" asked Dotty.

Natalie examined her nails as she replied. "It was lunchtime. Where else would they be?"

"Why don't we all visit The Orangery?" Dotty suggested.

"Is that really necessary?" sighed Natalie.

"Since we're here, we might as well complete the reconstruction," directed Nick.

They followed Dotty out of the hotel, across the tarmac drive and along the gravel path to The Orangery.

"It's closed," announced Keely in a disappointed tone.

"It's only open in the summer," Dotty explained. "But the restaurant was so busy during the antique fair that they hastily opened it up for light meals. You couldn't have arranged to meet your friends here, Natalie. None of you would have known it was open."

"I think I looked in the restaurant," stammered Natalie, "and heard someone mention The Orangery. That's it. Linda and Julie weren't in the restaurant, so I went to look for them in The Orangery."

"That might have happened," considered Dotty. "But you might already have known The Orangery was open when you passed it."

"What do you mean?" asked Keya.

"A footpath runs alongside The Orangery, and down to the valley below," explained Dotty.

"Oh, that one," acknowledged Keya. "We reached it from the car park next door."

Dotty glanced across at Natalie and saw the veins protruding on her neck as she clenched and unclenched her hands into fists.

"But it's not easy to get to that car park, is it, Keya?"

Keya shook her head. "We tried and failed in our cars."

Dotty continued, "But Norman was OK in his Land Rover. A 4x4 can access it."

Ryan and Keely both looked confused, but Nick was nodding his head in understanding.

Dotty knew it was time to drive home her advantage. "I don't think many people use the footpath, not in January, but I noticed a figure pass the window of The Orangery when I was inside. A figure wearing a grey hoodie, with the hood up."

Keya gasped. "Like that woman last night, at Lemington Village Hall. I swear she stole a bottle of gin."

"She did," confirmed Dotty. "And she works as a beautician in Cirencester. At the salon you own, Natalie."

Natalie shrugged. "So?"

"And she wore the same type of hoodie you wore when you parked next door and followed the footpath back to the antique fair." Dotty removed the hoodie she'd taken from Natalie's car and held it up. "This one."

Keely clapped her hands together. "That was just like the movies." She turned to Ryan, who smiled back at her, and nodded in agreement.

"Are you accusing me of murdering my husband because of a grey hoodie?" Natalie laughed, but there was a nervous note to it.

"And the missing star-shaped brooch? Which," she turned to Keya, "I think you'll find Edith has in a blue Wedgwood box in her room at the nursing home. I bet when you question her, she'll admit she picked it up somewhere near Roger's stall on the day he was killed."

"So what if I lost my brooch? It happens." Natalie widened her stance.

Keely stepped forward. She was shivering beneath her thin top. She glared at Natalie and confronted her. "You knew about me and Roger, didn't you? That's why you started shouting at me at the fair, rather than asking who I was. You didn't need to. You knew."

"This is all rubbish. I'm going home." Natalie turned and strode away down the path.

Dotty handed Natalie's car keys to Nick. "She won't get far without these."

Nick smiled at her. "Thank you. That was quite a performance, but I'm not sure we'll be able to convict her on that evidence alone. But we might find traces of blood on her hoodie."

Ryan held open a large transparent bag and Dotty dropped the hoodie into it.

"And there are walking boots in her car. I'm not sure if she'll have used them when she killed her husband, but it might be worth examining them for blood."

They finally caught up with Natalie at the hotel reception, where she was trying to order a taxi.

Nick stepped up to her and declared, "Natalie Wright, I'm arresting you for the murder of Roger Dewhirst ..."

Dotty heard a click and turned to watch Ozzie Winters, the young reporter with spiky black hair, take another photo and then speak into her phone. Was she talking to someone or recording herself? Dotty thought the latter.

Nick handed Ryan Natalie's car keys. "Can you drive Mrs Wright's car to the station? I'll escort her in the squad car. Keya, you better wait with Keely. Take her statement again and call for another car to take her home." He turned to Keely and said, "Thank you for your time, Miss Clarke."

Keely sniffed. "That's all right. If it helped catch Roger's killer." The fun and playfulness of earlier had disappeared. She probably realised the seriousness of what they'd been doing, and the consequences.

"Ryan, can you take Mrs Wright to the car?" asked Nick.

"Let go of me," squawked Natalie, as Ryan gripped her arm. Everyone in the reception and seating area stopped to watch.

Ozzie was talking quickly into her phone, her eyes taking in the whole scene.

Nick took Dotty's arm and led her to one side. "Thank you for all your help. You were incredible today. And we'll follow up all the leads.

Whether or not we'll have enough evidence for court, I believe we've arrested Roger Dewhirst's killer."

"That's OK." A warm glow spread through Dotty.

"Look," continued Nick. "Why don't you come round for supper one night?"

"I'm going away with work on Friday."

"Well, when you return."

Dotty's eyes met Nick's. "I'd like that."

CHAPTER FORTY-ONE

Dotty popped into Akemans on her way back from Charbury Castle Hotel and found a note, with a coffee stain on one corner, scribbled on her desk. Gilly must have left it.

She read, 'Marion coming tomorrow to sort out outfits for your trip to Istanbul. How exciting!'

She spent half an hour going through emails. Someone wanted to know if an oak sideboard, which hadn't sold at the last auction, was still available. That was a question for George, so she forwarded the message.

There were other enquiries about February's auction which she answered and with a sigh of satisfaction, she switched off her computer, made sure the front office door was locked and left via the antiques centre.

Norman must have heard her arrive home as he emerged from the barn and called, "Go through to the kitchen. Beanie is dying to speak to you. I'll be along in a minute."

"Come and sit down, and tell me all about this afternoon while I make you a cup of tea," welcomed Aunt Beanie. "The station was buzzing with news of Natalie Wright's arrest, and I know you were involved. Your photo is on the internet."

"It is?" asked Dotty, in surprise.

Aunt Beanie tapped her phone and passed it to Dotty. The main photograph, accompanying the article about Natalie's arrest for the murder of her husband, was of Ryan leading the suspect through the hotel's reception area, but there was a smaller one of Dotty talking to Nick.

"A great result, congratulations," enthused Aunt Beanie as she placed a cup of tea in front of Dotty.

Dotty was scrolling through the article to find who'd written it. She found the information at the end. Ozzie Winters was credited with taking the photos as well as writing the article.

"She must have been following us," Dotty reflected.

"Who?" asked Aunt Beanie, sitting down.

"That journalist, Ozzie Winters. This picture was taken outside the hotel when we were walking through the events at the craft fair." Dotty had found a third photo of Keya, Ryan and Keely. "I thought she just happened to be in the hotel reception and saw her opportunity and took it."

Aunt Beanie grinned. "Maybe she's heard of your detective prowess and is stalking you."

Dotty knew Aunt Beanie was joking, but it was still disconcerting.

Norman arrived in the kitchen and announced, "All done. Although Agatha is off her food. I'm not sure what's wrong."

"She's probably missing me and the warmth of the kitchen," replied Aunt Beanie. "Help yourself to tea. I've just made a fresh pot, and Dotty's about to tell us how she worked out Natalie Wright killed her husband."

Dotty told her story with only minimal interruptions from Aunt Beanie.

When she finished Norman sat back and praised, "Great deductive work, although I can see the police's point. There isn't much physical evidence. Weren't there any fingerprints on the murder weapon?"

"I'm not sure," replied Dotty. "But if there were, they'll have someone to match them with now."

Aunt Beanie was cradling her cup of tea. "Of course, this arrest doesn't appear to help with poor Ethel's case. Was Natalie Wright at the Malvern Fair?"

"I don't think so. I didn't see her, but I'm sure the police will check."

"But you don't think the deaths are linked, do you?" pressed Aunt Beanie.

Dotty shook her head. "Natalie's was a crime of passion, although Ethel might have seen her commit it, and Natalie needed to silence her. But I don't think that happened."

"One down, one to go," murmured Aunt Beanie.

"Except Ethel's case is officially with Worcestershire Police, so I don't think there's much Nick or his team can do." Dotty sipped her tea, and then asked, "What about you? Why were you in the office today?"

"We're trying to track down the chapan robe which was stolen at the Malvern Fair. Although that's also in Worcestershire's jurisdiction, they don't have a specialist team, so they've passed it on to us. We don't think the robe has left the country yet, but we've been tipped off it might soon, and we hope to seize it before it does."

"That's great news." Dotty yawned. "Oh, and I forgot to tell you. I've been invited by David's clients, or colleagues, I'm not sure which, to accompanying them on a trip to Istanbul to visit an international antique fair."

"That sounds very exciting. When is it?" asked Aunt Beanie.

"We're leaving on Friday."

"Not much time to get organised." Aunt Beanie raised an eyebrow.

"No, but Marion's going to help me."

On Wednesday morning, Marion arrived at nine o'clock. Dotty was pleased she'd had a chance to answer the few emails that had arrived overnight, and also to action the message George had sent replying to the enquiry about the unsold oak sideboard.

She emailed the seller and asked for their instructions and if they did still want to sell it, what was the minimum price they'd accept.

As Dotty finished, the fragrant smell of cardamom reached her and it became stronger as Marion placed her cup of coffee, infused with the spice, on the reception desk. Marion carried over the spare chair and sat opposite Dotty.

"You'll be away three days. Two for the fair and an extra one for sightseeing. Istanbul is a wonderful city," enthused Marion.

"Unfortunately, Ahmad Kazems' plane has developed a fault but his fellow countryman has offered you all a lift in his. Hopefully, the Kazem's plane will be fixed in time to fly you and David home. But what it does mean is that all your luggage has to be packed and brought to the office tomorrow morning. They're sending a car to collect it."

It all sounded very organised, but rather daunting.

"Will I be the only female on the trip?" asked Dotty.

"No, Tariq's younger sister, Nadia, will be on the plane, but I don't think she's staying long in Istanbul. Perhaps just the weekend like you."

Marion sipped her coffee before continuing. "Now, it's actually quite cold in Istanbul at this time of year, around ten degrees. So a couple of smart trouser suits with long-sleeved blouses or a long dress with leggings underneath and long sleeves will be ideal for the fair. You'll need to wear a scarf as well and be prepared to cover your head with it if someone asks you to. And for the evening, you'll need to dress up but also keep your arms, legs and chest covered up. Do you have any long-sleeved tunic tops?"

Dotty thought about her wardrobe, which she'd slowly been expanding. She knew she had a suitable dress and trouser suit, but she wasn't sure about tunics.

"I might, but I've no idea if they are long or short-sleeved, and I don't think they're very smart."

"Never mind." Marion smiled and confided, "Just the excuse we need to go shopping. And as David said, he's charging the Kazems for your outfits, so let's go to Cheltenham for the morning."

Dotty glanced at her computer. "But what about my work here?"

"We'll be back this afternoon, after we've enjoyed a pleasant lunch, and I'll come in tomorrow and help, so you and David can prepare for the fair."

Dotty didn't return to work. Marion had insisted she had her hair trimmed and her hands manicured.

Dotty didn't think either was really necessary, but she enjoyed her manicure, although the assistant was disappointed when she asked for a clear nail varnish, rather than a bright colour.

"What do you think?" she asked Aunt Beanie and Norman as she paraded through the kitchen wearing a new black and gold tunic top with black leggings and a gold jacket and scarf.

"Black doesn't suit you," remarked Aunt Beanie. "But at least the gold of the scarf and jacket breaks it up."

"I think you look very smart," comforted Norman, throwing Aunt Beanie a reproachful glance.

"The main point is to fit in and not cause offence," explained Dotty. "If nobody notices or comments on what I'm wearing, that'll be a good thing. Now I better go and pack my new outfits and everything else I need for the trip. It's being collected tomorrow, ready for my flight on Friday."

"Are you flying from Heathrow?" asked Norman.

"No, Cotswold Airport, on a private jet."

Dotty grinned but faltered as she noticed a shadow cross Aunt Beanie's face.

The older woman looked at her and said, without enthusiasm, "That'll be an experience."

CHAPTER FORTY-TWO

It was bright but chilly when Dotty and David arrived at Cotswold Airport early on Friday morning in a black chauffeur-driven Mercedes.

"As-salamu alaikum," greeted Tariq as he walked across and held his hand out to David who shook it.

To Dotty he asked, "Are you excited about your trip?"

She nodded and blew on her hands to warm them up. She had a pair of black leather gloves, but she'd packed them in her suitcase.

"My father and his friends will arrive shortly, so if you'd like to identify your bags, they can be loaded onto the plane."

Tariq pointed to a white jet parked close by. As they watched, a hatch door opened behind the long cone-shaped nose and a blue clad steward appeared as a set of steps automatically extended towards the ground.

"If you'll come with me," instructed Tariq with a smile.

"That's mine." Dotty pointed to a black case standing on wheels whose handle was already extended.

David pointed to a brown leather holdall.

"Thank you. Now we can board," declared Tariq.

Dotty lifted the small green holdall which contained her handbag, wash bag and electronic items. She could hear the wheels of her suitcase trundling along the tarmac and she turned to watch a blue overalled man lift it up and slide it into a cargo area towards the rear of the plane.

She took hold of the balustrade and was about to step onto the bottom step when bright spotlights lit up the scene and a voice, amplified by a megaphone, shouted, "Stop there and put your hands on your heads."

Dotty froze. Her heart pumping madly in her chest and her hand still on the balustrade.

"I repeat. Put your hands on your heads."

Dotty felt David move beside her, so she pulled her leg back and lifted both her hands above her head. This was not the exciting and luxurious plane trip she'd been expecting.

Dotty waited for at least an hour on her own in an interview room in Cirencester police station. It was just as soulless as when she'd sat in it before Christmas, before she was interviewed about a mystery suitcase and trip to Vienna.

A trip she'd never taken. She had a feeling she wasn't going to experience Istanbul either.

Glumly, she considered the only furniture in the room. A grey Formica table, with some sort of electronic recording device on it, and four black chairs. Even the walls were grey.

Was she doomed never to take trips abroad? Three times now she'd talked about or planned trips which hadn't happened and this was the second time she'd been arrested before she'd even left.

The door opened and Aunt Beanie bustled in carrying a paper cup and a bacon sandwich wrapped in a white paper napkin.

"Ryan called and told me you'd been arrested, but I can't speak about that. I thought you'd be hungry, as you won't have had breakfast and a cup of tea is always welcome."

"Thank you," replied Dotty gratefully as Aunt Beanie placed her offerings on the table and stood silently watching Dotty.

"I just know there's been some mistake," cried Aunt Beanie, and she turned and rushed from the room.

Dotty slowly munched her sandwich. Not really tasting it, but at least it was something to do. The tea, which she was sure contained half a spoon of sugar, was very welcome.

She was down to the last dregs of tea when the door opened and a smartly dressed man walked in. Dotty hadn't seen him before. He was in his thirties with tawny coloured skin, a shaved head and a pencil moustache.

"Dorothy, how are they treating you? I'm Omar Farsi and Ahmad Kazem has sent me to represent you."

Dotty felt her chest tighten as she replied, "Um … Why?" She knew it didn't sound very sophisticated or grateful, but she was utterly confused. "I mean, what am I doing here? And why does Mr Ahmad feel he needs to provide me with a solicitor?"

"I gather it was Tariq's idea," admitted Mr Farsi. "As you were arrested under his charge, he feels responsible for you. Besides, I came to advocate for David Rook."

"Has David been arrested?"

The lawyer placed a slim, black leather briefcase on the table and sat down.

"No, but he is helping the police with their enquiries. As to why you've been arrested, it appears an expensive chapan robe was found in your luggage. One that had recently been stolen."

Dotty gasped. "At the Malvern Antique Fair."

"So you know the item the police are referring to?"

"Yes, I saw it displayed on the wall of a stall. It was beautiful. Purple silk with silver and gold brocade."

Mr Farsi opened his suitcase and removed a photograph. He placed it on the table and turned it round to face Dotty. "This one?"

"Yes, that's it. Someone stole it on the Saturday, around the time poor Ethel was killed. But why do the police think I took it?"

Mr Farsi returned the photograph to his case. "You've admitted you were there, and that you recognise the item."

"Because David and I saw some at an auction in London," interjected Dotty, her voice rising.

"And it was found in your suitcase, which was loaded onto the plane this morning."

Dotty blinked. "It was what?"

"Are you denying you packed it in your suitcase?"

"Of course I am. I didn't take it." She knew she sounded hysterical. She breathed deeply, trying to calm herself down.

"And has the suitcase been out of your sight since you packed it?"

Dotty nodded. "Yes. A car collected it from Akemans yesterday and I didn't see it again until Tariq asked me to identify it at the airport this morning."

"Did anyone see it leave?"

Dotty thought back to Thursday. She, Gilly and Marion had been discussing Istanbul in the back of the office when the uniformed chauffeur had knocked on the locked door of the auction house.

Gilly had agreed she could unlock the front door and let him in. Dotty had wheeled her suitcase across and he'd picked it up and carried it outside. She remembered hoping she'd packed everything she needed.

"Yes, both Marion Rook and Gilly Wimsey saw me hand it over to a uniformed chauffeur."

"Excellent." Mr Farsi snapped shut his briefcase. "No clear chain of evidence. It might not be enough for the police to drop the charges, but at least I can get you out of here."

CHAPTER FORTY-THREE

Mr Farsi left and Dotty sat on her own for another half an hour or so before Chief Inspector Ringrose entered.

He placed another paper cup of tea on the table together with some papers and said, "Bernadette insisted I bring you this, and," he placed a white paper napkin on the table which opened to reveal a chocolate brownie and two digestive biscuits, "young PC Jenkins sent you these. He's quite a fan of yours."

Despite the seriousness of her situation, Dotty smiled. At least she had someone who still supported her. Who believed in her.

The chief inspector removed his blue wool suit jacket and placed it over the back of the chair nearest the wall, then sat down opposite Dotty. He clicked the recording device and said, "Friday third of February. Twelve-fifteen."

Dotty realised she'd been sitting in the interview room longer than she thought, and having only eaten a bacon sandwich, she reached forward and picked up a digestive biscuit.

"Present are Chief Inspector Ringrose and the suspect." He looked up at Dotty. "Please state your full name."

"Dorothy Lavender Sayers."

The chief inspector raised his eyebrows. Was it her middle name which had surprised him?

"Mrs Sayers, you have been cautioned, but do you understand why you've been arrested?"

"Not really," she admitted.

The chief inspector picked up the papers and read. "At 06.30 today you were apprehended boarding a flight to Istanbul. You were observed pointing to a suitcase which was loaded onto the same plane. A suitcase in which we found a missing Oriental robe."

"Middle Eastern, not Oriental," corrected Dotty.

"Quite right." Chief Inspector Ringrose removed a pen from his inside jacket pocket and made a note on the sheet of paper.

"This robe, known as a chapan, was stolen from Timeless Treasures who had it on display at their stall at Bishop's Antique Fair, near Malvern, Worcestershire."

"That's right," said Dotty. "On the Saturday. And I did admire it at the fair, but I didn't steal it. I was with Sergeants Unwin and Varma, searching for suspects in the Roger Dewhirst case, and after poor Ethel was killed, I drove Edith home."

"But you weren't with my colleagues all the time, were you?"

"No," admitted Dotty. "We split up for our search, but not for long. That's when I saw the chapan, still hanging on the baize partition of the stall in the room where I later found Ethel."

"And when you found Ethel's body, there must have been quite a commotion. Enough for you to sneak into the stall and steal the robe?"

Dotty blinked rapidly. Did the chief inspector think her that callous?

"I'd just discovered a dead body. The last thing on my mind was a Middle Eastern robe. As soon as I found Ethel, I went in search of Nick, Sergeant Unwin, and we returned to the room together. Then Keya, Sergeant Varma, began interviewing the people who were in the stall and Sergeant Unwin asked me to go back to the fair entrance and make sure nobody else came in or left."

Chief Inspector Ringrose tapped the top of the table with his pen. "Did you see the robe when you discovered Ethel's body?"

"No, but I wasn't exactly looking for it."

"In fact, nobody seems to have seen it since you told Sergeant Varma you did, when conducting your search."

"It doesn't mean it wasn't there," countered Dotty, beginning to feel angry at the injustice of her arrest. "Did someone see me take it?"

"No," admitted the chief inspector, "But that doesn't mean you didn't."

"But why would I want it? It isn't something I'd wear walking around the Cotswolds."

"I don't know. It wasn't dissimilar to other items we found in your suitcase."

"Which I bought with Marion Rook in Cheltenham, to wear in Istanbul. Do you think I was going to wear the jacket there?"

Chief Inspector Ringrose sighed. "No, I don't think you were going to wear it. It's too valuable. I believe it was being shipped to Istanbul for a client. What I don't know is if you are involved or if, once again, you are an innocent party."

Dotty slumped back in her seat. He was right. It was the second time valuable stolen items had been found in her bags. She'd managed to persuade the police the first time that she knew nothing about them, but would they believe her a second time?

"So you can see my dilemma. On the face of it, you're up to your neck stealing and smuggling antiques, but on the other hand, Bernadette is protesting your innocence. And, as your lawyer has pointed out, your suitcase was out of your possession for nearly a day, so there was ample opportunity for someone else to tamper with it. So what to do?" He tapped the table again with his pen.

Dotty held her breath as she watched the chief inspector.

He lifted his pen. "You're free to go. For now."

Dotty pushed back her chair.

"Stay here. I'll ask PC Jenkins to escort you out."

As the chief inspector opened the door of the interview room, she heard Aunt Beanie demand, "Are you letting her go? You're out of you mind if you think she's mixed up in Operation Bumblebee."

"Shh," uttered Chief Inspector Ringrose as he closed the door.

Operation Bumblebee. Now that was interesting.

A few minutes later, Ryan opened the door and smiled at her apologetically. "I'm sorry about all this."

"Don't worry, it isn't your fault." Dotty stood up.

"And you've missed your trip to Istanbul?"

"Have I?" queried Dotty.

"Yes, the plane left two hours ago with the Kazems on board."

"What about David Rook?"

"He left twenty minutes ago with his solicitor, Mr Farsi."

So much for representing her.

She walked slowly down the corridor in front of Ryan. Up ahead, she spotted Nick standing in a doorway. He watched her for several seconds before turning and entering the room, pushing past Keya as she stepped into the corridor.

As Dotty approached, Keya whispered, "Are you OK?"

"To be truthful, I'm not really sure. It was a shock being arrested, but now it's the way people look at me. As if I am guilty. That's what really hurts."

Keya looked down at the floor. "You mean Nick. I saw the disappointed look on his face."

"I'm sure he'll come round," offered Ryan. "And we know you're not involved."

Keya looked up, grinning. "And so does Aunt Beanie. She's been creating quite a fuss this morning."

"What's Operation Bumblebee?"

Keya and Ryan exchanged glances.

"Above our pay grade to speak about that," confessed Ryan.

"Come on, I'll walk with you," offered Keya. "Aunt Beanie and Norman are waiting for you outside."

CHAPTER FORTY-FOUR

Dotty kept herself to herself on Saturday, remaining in her own cottage rather than venturing through to the main farmhouse.

She suspected Earl Grey had no such qualms. He leapt off the sofa where she lay, wrapped in a blanket watching Bargain Hunt, and disappeared. Most likely he'd gone through to beg Aunt Beanie for food as a wonderful aroma of freshly baked fruit tart drifted through to Dotty's cottage.

He eventually returned with a note tied around his front leg and appeared grateful when Dotty removed it.

He curled up at her feet as she read, 'I'll leave you be today, but you have to face the world sometime. Norman is going to finish the Drover's Trail tomorrow. Can you drive him to his starting point while I visit Cliff? And will you help me cook an early evening Sunday roast? I've already made a pie and done the cauliflower cheese. I'll invite Keya, Ryan and Nick along to give us an update, and I'll ask one of them to pick Norman up if he makes it to Evesham. Sleep Well. B.'

Surprisingly, Dotty did sleep well, and she felt refreshed on Sunday morning. She opened her daisy-patterned curtains, soaking in the soft sunshine outside. Today was a new day.

She knew people were judging her and some believed she was guilty of trying to smuggle a valuable stolen artefact out of the country.

But she was innocent. Her integrity and values would not allow her to commit such a crime. And perhaps facing her own truth, with honesty and sincerity, was to know herself.

Perhaps that was the essence of understanding and self-awareness that Norman was searching for. She was happy being herself, with her own identity, however others judged her.

She showered and dressed and arrived in the kitchen of the main farmhouse as Norman was filling his black metal water bottle.

"Are you OK to give me a lift?" he asked.

Dotty smiled and replied, "Ready when you are."

As they drove along the winding Cotswold lanes, Dotty noticed more patches of snowdrops and even a few purple and orange crocuses.

"I love spring," she admitted. "It's all about new beginnings."

"Is it?" asked Norman. "Or are we just going round in circles?"

"Why do you say that?"

"Each year we keep thinking things will improve, but new obstacles are thrown in our way. Take you, for example. You're just getting over one disappointment and feeling of betrayal, and moving forward, when someone else sets you up and you're arrested."

"What are you getting at, Norman?"

"I don't know," he mused. "But the more I, we, strive towards truth, knowledge, and enlightenment, the more I feel we're drawn into a tangled web of deceit. How well do we really know those around us?"

"That's rather profound for a Sunday morning. Have you been reading too much Victor Frankl?"

"You might jest, young lady. But I'm just warning you. Be careful."

Dotty shivered and her earlier optimism faded a little. She hated to admit that Norman's words unsettled her.

She dropped Norman off at Buckland, close to the edge of the

Cotswold escarpment, and shouted, "Good luck," as he disappeared along a stony track.

The Defender was parked in the yard when she returned to Meadowbank Farm and she found Aunt Beanie in the kitchen, reading the Sunday papers.

Dotty asked, "How was Uncle Cliff?"

"Not great. He didn't recognise me at all today, so I didn't stay long. Edith came to say hello, and she said she would sit with Cliff after I left. She was asking after you."

"You didn't tell her I'd been arrested for stealing and smuggling, did you?" Dotty asked in a despondent voice.

"No I did not," replied Aunt Beanie primly. "And you're fortunate, there's no mention of your arrest in the Sunday papers. But your friend, Ozzie Winters ..."

"She's not my friend. I hardly know her," interjected Dotty.

"Well, she's done very nicely for herself. Not only is there her report on the arrest of Natalie Wright, but another article speculating about a link between Roger's death and Ethel's."

"She's probably making more progress than Worcestershire Police," Dotty muttered.

"Why? How far have they got?"

"Not very, I believe, but we'll have to ask our police friends this evening."

Dotty peeled potatoes and helped prepare carrots and spinach for supper.

"You've been a great help, thank you," said Aunt Beanie. "Why don't you sit down and finish reading the papers or watch TV? I've just got the lamb to prepare, and I'll pop it into the oven shortly."

Dotty glanced at her phone as she sat down at the kitchen table. It was four o'clock.

"We haven't heard from Norman," Aunt Beanie remarked. "Or Ryan, who's offered to pick him up. I hope he's OK."

"This is interesting," said Dotty, reading the paper. "It says that a reward has been offered for information about Bernard Ingram, who's been working as a member of the ground staff at Cotswold Airport. It says his wife reported him missing yesterday, after he didn't return home from work on Friday."

She looked up at Aunt Beanie. "You don't think this is linked to my case, do you?"

"I'm sure I couldn't say," replied Aunt Beanie, opening the fridge door and hiding behind it.

"And I wonder who's put up the reward?"

Aunt Beanie didn't reply.

The door opened and Keya, Ryan and bedraggled but smiling Norman, walked in.

"There you are," exclaimed Aunt Beanie in relief.

"I just had a few drinks to celebrate," admitted Norman, swaying slightly.

"You're drunk," announced Aunt Beanie. "Come on, you need a bath, or a cold shower." As she dragged Norman out of the kitchen, she called, "Dotty, can you put the lamb in the oven?"

"Poor Norman," giggled Keya. "But it got me thinking. Was Natalie Wright a walker? Otherwise, how did she know about that car park next to the hotel? It was hidden away."

Dotty stood up. "I'm sure she mentioned it when we first saw her sitting in the hotel bar. She said something about being happy for Roger to attend fairs and leave her to her walking."

Keya nodded. "Yes, I think you're right." She placed a yellow plastic bag on the worktop and pulled out a leek and cheese pie. "I told Aunt Beanie I'd bring my own main course."

As Dotty reached the worktop, she looked from Keya to Ryan and asked in a small voice, "Is Nick joining us?"

Keya shuffled her feet.

Ryan stepped forward and said, "I believe you had nothing to do with that stolen robe, and so does Keya, but Nick, well, he thinks there's no smoke without fire."

"What he actually said," admitted Keya, "is that you're either naïve or guilty to be caught trying to smuggle stolen items out of the country again."

Dotty opened her mouth, but Keya cut in. "I know. Gilmore was found guilty, and it's very suspicious a member of the ground crew went missing the very day you were arrested, but Nick thinks too highly of you. Give him time. I'm sure he'll come round."

"I looked into the missing man, Bernard Ingram's finances today," admitted Ryan.

Keya narrowed her eyes at him.

Ryan shook his head. "Don't ask how. But I discovered £5,000 was transferred to his bank account on Thursday."

"That is interesting," mused Keya. "Isn't it, Dotty?"

Dotty poked the final sprig of rosemary into one of the many slits that punctured the surface of the leg of lamb. "I suppose so," she muttered and opening the top door of the oven, she slid the joint of lamb inside.

CHAPTER FORTY-FIVE

Aunt Beanie looked around the kitchen table. Norman was freshly bathed and had sobered up enough to carve the tender joint of lamb. Ryan was salivating as his hands hovered over his knife and fork.

Aunt Beanie prayed, "Dear Lord, thank you for bringing us together to share your bounty. Bless those who are unable to join us and protect those who are vulnerable. Amen."

"Amen," murmured everyone else.

Aunt Beanie announced, "Dotty was reading an article by that young journalist, Ozzie Winters, speculating about a link between Roger's death and Ethel's. What do you think, Ryan?"

"Worcestershire Police haven't made a connection," he replied simply.

"I doubt they've been looking for one," muttered Keya. "Hey, I forgot to tell you with all the excitement on Friday."

Dotty hadn't found it at all exciting.

"The development company was granted planning permission for the redevelopment of Jasmine Street and Hyacinth Crescent. Demolition is due to start immediately."

"Poor Ethel, what's happened to her cats?" asked Aunt Beanie.

"They're at the local rescue centre and five of them have already been adopted," Ryan revealed.

"That's great news." Aunt Beanie sipped the red wine Ryan had brought. She grimaced slightly, and Dotty wondered if it wasn't as high quality as the bottle Nick had brought the previous Sunday.

Dotty was sticking to water and as she picked up her glass, she wondered out loud, "What will happen to her possessions?"

"I've failed to find a next of kin or a will, so the council will go in next week and clear her house," remarked Ryan as he cut into a slice of lamb.

Aunt Beanie wrinkled her forehead before asking, "Do you still have a set of keys to Ethel's house?"

Ryan finished chewing and replied hesitantly, "Yes, I do."

"I think I might accidentally borrow them on Monday. And Dotty, I don't think you should go into the office. Have a day off and collect Edith and go for a drive."

"In the direction of Gloucester?" she asked, picking up Aunt Beanie's train of thought.

"It'll give her closure, to finally see where her friend lived, and maybe she'll find something to remember her by."

"No need to borrow the keys. I need to interview Edith about the star-shaped brooch. Perhaps you can help me, Dotty? She might be more forthcoming with you. And maybe she'll be able to shed some light on Ethel's death by visiting her house."

Aunt Beanie clasped her hands together. "That's settled. Ryan, you pick Dotty up at nine and visit Edith, and take her to Gloucester."

Ryan looked down at his plate before he admitted, "And then I have the rest of the week off."

"Going somewhere nice?" asked Norman.

Ryan turned pink as he admitted, "I've taken Keya's advice and enrolled on a beginners cookery course at Hilcot Manor."

"Good man," congratulated Norman.

"Excellent idea," agreed Aunt Beanie. "Oh, and I forgot to tell you, Dotty, that I read an interesting article while you were out this morning. About those clay tiles you and David were called to authenticate at the beginning of January."

"The ones in the British Museum?" queried Dotty.

"They're there at the moment, but the Iraqi government has submitted another formal request for them to be returned to their country of origin, and they're trying to gather international support."

"I wonder how long that discussion will go on for," said Keya.

"The British Museum might say it's opposed to the illegal trade of artefacts, but it's displaying an awful lot of treasures from an array of different cultures. And talking of petitions, and returning property," Keya looked at Ryan, "didn't you say Quinn's parents have lodged a request for the return of their investment?"

"That's right," agreed Ryan, "But I'm not sure how long they'll have to wait for Roger's estate to be resolved."

"There goes Quinn's next business venture," remarked Keya.

"It's certainly been a mixed week," admitted Aunt Beanie. "I just hope enough evidence is found to convict Natalie Wright."

"We're still struggling with physical evidence," conceded Ryan.

"Her fingerprints weren't on the toasting fork, but Keya's prints were smudged, which suggested someone wore gloves. And we found a pair of white cotton ones in the back of Natalie's car. Apparently dealers use them when handling items like glass so they don't leave finger marks. I'm trying to see if I can link them to the murder weapon."

Dotty felt her phone vibrate, and she removed it from her pocket. "It's a message from George suggesting I take a few days off. Marion will cover the office as David's left on a trip."

"Already," remarked Aunt Beanie. "And he didn't offer to take you this time. I wonder where he's gone?"

CHAPTER FORTY-SIX

Dotty was waiting for Ryan on Monday morning as he drove through the entrance of Windrush Farm in his black car.

Twenty-five minutes later they arrived at Burford Care Home and were met in the entrance hall by Mrs Richardson, the care home manager.

She was young for such a responsibility, about Dotty's own age, and she had an open, round face and light brown hair. She frowned slightly when she saw Dotty. "I was expecting the police, but aren't you Cliff Devereux's niece?"

Dotty didn't correct Mrs Richardson. Aunt Beanie had originally introduced Dotty as her niece, as it was easier than explaining their actual relationship.

"She's helping me today," explained Ryan. "Constable Jenkins, and I've come to interview Edith Jessop. And if she feels up to it, I'd like to take her to her friend Ethel's house, to help us with our enquiries."

"You won't upset her, will you?" asked Mrs Richardson sharply.

"No," soothed Ryan. "That's why Mrs Sayers is with me."

"Very well." Mrs Richardson led them to Edith's first-floor room and, opening the door, she said, "Edith, here are the visitors I told you about."

Edith was sitting in a chair by the window, staring out. When she turned towards them, she beamed and replied, "I'm so grateful. I didn't know what I was going to do with myself all week, with no chance of escape at the weekend."

Mrs Richardson's nose wrinkled in disapproval. "I'll leave you to it," she said stiffly. "Please sign Edith out with the receptionist and back in again on her return. No more sneaking out, Edith."

Edith grinned as Mrs Richardson left, closing the door behind her. "I ordered tea and coffee, but I'm not sure it'll arrive. But someone said we might be going out." Edith's bright eyes stared at Dotty.

"All in good time, Mrs Jessop," replied Ryan.

"Miss, and anyway, everyone calls me Edith. Dotty, sit here, and young man, why don't you bring over another chair? I didn't know how many people to expect."

Dotty moved her chair closer to the window, making room for Ryan, who sat down on the mahogany stool from the dressing table.

Ryan said, "Edith, I'm not sure if you know, but Natalie Wright has been arrested for the murder of her husband, Roger."

Edith nodded her head enthusiastically. "Beanie told me. And she said you were the clever one who worked it all out." She leaned across and patted Dotty's knee.

"It was a team effort," insisted Dotty, blushing.

"Edith, Dotty told us you have a star-shaped diamond brooch. Can you tell me about it?"

"I ... I ..." Edith dipped her chin and looked down at the floor.

"It's OK, Edith. Nobody's accusing you of anything," reassured Dotty. "But I saw Natalie wearing a similar brooch at the antique fair, and I wondered if she'd dropped it and you'd picked it up."

Edith cleared her throat and looked up at Dotty. "I did find it. On the floor at the side of Roger's stall. When Roger's body was discovered, everyone crowded around. Everyone except Ethel, that is. And that's when I saw it, lying on the ground. I knew it wasn't from Roger's stall as he didn't sell jewellery, and I did mean to find out whose it was. It's just that ..." Her voice trailed off.

"It's just that so much has happened," finished Dotty. "Don't worry. But do you mind if I get it and give it to Ryan? It's evidence in Roger's case."

Edith nodded her agreement.

Dotty stood and walked across to the glass-fronted case on top of the bureau and removed the blue Wedgwood trinket box. Fishing about inside she found and removed the star-shaped diamond brooch. "It is pretty, and I suspect these are real diamonds."

"Honestly, I only thought it was costume jewellery," insisted Edith, as Dotty handed the brooch to Ryan.

The scene at Jasmine Street, where Ethel had lived was depressing. Preparations for demolition were already underway and Ryan had needed to call ahead to get permission to visit.

A workman wearing a yellow high-vis jacket and hard hat met them at the entrance to the street and opened a section of the metal fencing which surrounded the site. Ryan drove forward and parked outside number five.

Unlike the other houses, the front door had been painted in the last few years, although flecks of blue were starting to peel off now.

Inside, the house smelt of damp and neglect. The worn dark red carpet, with abstract floral motifs, must have dated back to the 1960s or 1970s, and Dotty suspected the threadbare armchairs in the living room were from the same period. And everything was covered in cat hairs.

"It's a good job Keya isn't here," Dotty mused. "She'd never had coped with all these cat hairs."

"Ethel really did love her cats," insisted Edith.

"Are we looking for anything in particular, Ryan?" asked Dotty.

"As no next of kin has been found, I thought Edith might see if there are any items she wants to keep to remember Ethel, while you and I look for anything which might be connected to Ethel's death."

They began their search.

Edith placed cat ornaments on a stained elm coffee table while Dotty and Ryan searched the rest of the room.

"It's all ornaments and cat toys in here," remarked Dotty. "Shall we try the next door?"

The next room was a small dining room with a hatch into the single-storey kitchen. Dotty suspected the bathroom would be beyond that, as the original terraced house would only have had an outside privy, or toilet in a shed.

The dining room contained a vintage elm sideboard which matched the coffee table in the living room. It might have been worth something except one leg was missing and had been replaced with a pile of browning magazines.

Dotty opened one of the sideboard's cupboards and a pile of magazines cascaded to the floor. She picked one up. It was an old edition of the Antiques Gazette.

She showed it to Ryan as he entered the room and said, "Ethel took her antiques seriously."

"I've just helped Edith up to the bedroom and there are some nice ornaments and knick-knacks. The room is very tidy, with the bed made and apart from a thin covering of dust, it looks as if Ethel's only just stepped out. I took a box up there with me and some old newspapers so Edith can wrap up the more delicate items."

"That was forward thinking," Dotty responded as she opened another cupboard door and removed a cardboard box with a faded picture of apples on the side. She carried it across to the small mahogany dining table.

"Look at this," she said to Ryan and handed him a newspaper clipping.

"This is the article Ozzie Winters wrote about Roger Dewhirst's death," observed Ryan. "Perhaps Ethel's death is linked to Roger's."

"I don't see how," replied Dotty. "Roger was killed by his wife because he was having an affair. It had nothing to do with Ethel."

The next clipping was about the copper jug, which had been stolen at Cotswold Antique Fair, being put on display at the National Museum of Iraq.

Dotty lifted up a bunch of clippings and noticed the one below was about a dagger at the same museum. A dagger she was sure she'd seen in the office of the commanding officer of her late husband's regiment.

"Do you mind if I take these to look through?" she asked, returning the clippings to the box.

"Why? Do you think there's something in there which will provide a motive for Ethel's death?"

"I'm not sure. It just looks like newspaper articles about antiques."

Dotty knew this wasn't entirely true, but she doubted anyone at Cirencester police station would have time to examine the contents properly, and Worcestershire Police must already have removed anything from the house they thought was relevant.

"OK, but if you do find something, please promise you'll tell me or Keya, and not go investigating on your own," insisted Ryan.

Dotty nodded her consent as she opened the final cupboard door. Inside there was a box of photos and photograph books. "And I'll take these. I can't bear to think of someone from the council throwing her memories in the skip."

Ryan helped Dotty carry the two boxes back to his car. They searched the rest of the house but found nothing else of interest.

"What do you think of this?" Edith asked as Dotty wrapped an attractive black feline shaped vase.

"Very pretty." It was a cat-shaped brooch with attractive multi-coloured stones.

"I think I'll keep this, as my memory of Ethel," said Edith, pocketing the brooch.

"And the rest?" asked Ryan as he picked up a box of newspaper wrapped items.

"I'll sell them and donate the profits to a cat charity. Beanie told me she's taking a table at a sale soon. Perhaps I'll be able to have one too."

"That sounds like an excellent idea," agreed Dotty.

Dotty settled Edith into Ryan's car before returning to stand beside him as he locked Ethel's front door.

"We didn't find much to help with Ethel's case," he remarked.

"I don't know," replied Dotty. "If you agree with me that it's not linked to Roger's death, then I don't think this is the end. It might take time, but I'm sure we will find out who killed her. You, me and Keya. We just need more time, and a few more pieces of the puzzle to fall into place."

CHAPTER FORTY-SEVEN

Dotty walked through the white marquee which had been erected in the garden at the rear of Windrush Hall, where various stallholders were setting up their displays.

"This is your table, Mrs Robinson," instructed Keya as she checked the clipboard she carried. "Yes, number nine."

It was the last Saturday in February and Dotty had taken advantage of Marion working in the office to help Keya prepare for the charity tabletop sale.

She had considered helping Aunt Beanie and Norman, who'd taken two tables, but Edith had asked Aunt Beanie, on one of her visits to see Uncle Cliff, if she could help and in return sell the small collection of items she'd rescued from Ethel's house.

"Pretty brooch," Dotty remarked.

Edith smiled at her. "I think Ethel would approve." Edith had pinned Ethel's fun, multicoloured cat brooch to her yellow jacket.

Dotty was pleased they had visited Ethel's house, as she'd recently seen pictures on the local news of the flattened site where it once stood.

Norman was arranging walking sticks, umbrellas and canes in a metal stand.

Dotty commented, "That works well."

"I'll sell the stand as well, if someone offers the right price, but don't tell Beanie," confided Norman.

"Don't tell Beanie what?" asked the older woman, who was arranging crockery. Keya had bought a large number of items, but those she hadn't, Beanie had brought to the sale.

"Morning, where shall I put these?" asked Ryan.

"Oh, a Victoria sponge," said Keya, peering into the transparent cake holder Ryan held.

"And there are fondant fancies and three Battenberg cakes in this basket," declared Ryan proudly.

Dotty took the cake from Ryan. "That's wonderful. Thank you so much. Let's take them into the house. You've clearly been practising after you finished your course."

Ryan blushed. "I attended a baking course last weekend."

"Good for you."

"It's fun," admitted Ryan. "And I've met some new people."

"Anyone in particular?" asked Dotty as they entered the dining room.

Ryan's face turned a darker shade of red.

"Don't worry, I'm only teasing."

They entered the dining room and started unpacking Ryan's cakes.

"Where do you want us to set up?" asked a familiar voice.

Dotty turned to face Keely and smiled. "Hello. Have you reserved a stall?"

"Yes, we have."

Quinn Hughes appeared in the doorway carrying a wooden box and puffing, "Glass is heavy."

"Don't you drop that," admonished Keely.

"The stalls are in the marquee in the garden at the back of the house. You can carry that box through, but you might find it easier to park in the courtyard at the side of the house and carry everything from there."

"Did you hear that, Quinn?" called Keely. "You can move the van to the courtyard and carry the boxes while I set up."

"Is Quinn helping you out?" asked Dotty.

"We've gone into business. I found a key to a lockup with more stock and," she lowered her voice to a whisper, "more cash. I felt sorry for Quinn's parents, Roger having taken their savings, so I gave some of the cash to them. And would you believe it? Quinn asked if he could invest it in the business with me. So here we are. Partners."

Keely turned and followed Quinn through the hall.

"Well, that's a turn up for the books," remarked Dotty to Ryan. "I presume you didn't hear anything about a lockup or cash?"

"What cash?" Ryan tried, but failed, to portray an innocent expression. "But I did notice Keely is taking her business seriously. She looked very smart in her brown suede trousers and fitted polo neck."

"Now," said Dotty. "Remember your girl from the cookery class."

Ryan blushed again.

Keya walked in and exclaimed, "This looks great!"

"And no irate villagers to throw my cakes around," declared Ryan.

Keya rolled her eyes. "Don't mention Lemington. They found a new campaign to unite them. And this time they might have a point."

Who did kill Ethel? Why are Keya's unruly inhabitants of Lemington important? Is Sergeant Unwin right to think Dotty is either guilty or naive to be caught smuggling stolen antiques out of the country again? Can Dotty get herself out of trouble this time?

A victim who dies twice. A web of deceit. With the help of her friends, can an amateur sleuth crack the case, or will she pay the ultimate price?

Claim your copy of Priceless Betrayal

Would you like to read about Dotty's first case, and discover why she joined Akemans?

Find out in the prequel, *Hour is Come,* when you sign up to my newsletter for updates.

Claim your Copy of Hour is Come

If you enjoyed this book, please tell someone you know. And for those people you don't know, leave a review to help them decide whether or not to read it.

For more information visit VictoriaTait.com

UNTITLED

UNTITLED

Printed in Great Britain
by Amazon

38393927R00129